The Slackers

Álvaro Cunhal's official military release, dated February 27, 1940.

The Slackers
and Other Stories

Manuel Tiago
(Álvaro Cunhal)

Translated and with a foreword by
Eric A. Gordon

INTERNATIONAL PUBLISHERS
New York

Copyright © Editorial «Avante!», 2021

First English language edition, 2021 by International Publishers Co., Inc. / NY by special arrangement with Editorial Avante!

Translated from the Portuguese by Eric A. Gordon © 2020
Foreword by Eric A. Gordon © 2020

Printed in the United States of America
All rights reserved

Except for brief passages for review purposes, no part of this book may be reproduced or transmitted in any form or by any means, electronic or mechanical, including photocopying, recording, or via any information storage retrieval system, without permission in writing from the publisher

Library of Congress Cataloging-in-Publication Data

Names: Tiago, Manuel, author. | Gordon, Eric A., 1945- translator, writer of foreword.
Title: The slackers : and other stories / Manuel Tiago (Álvaro Cunhal) ; translated and with a foreword by Eric A. Gordon.
Other titles: Preguiçosos. English
Description: First English language edition. | New York : International Publishers, 2021. | Summary: "The Slackers is a collection of short stories by Manuel Tiago"—Provided by publisher.
Identifiers: LCCN 2021039636 (print) | LCCN 2021039637 (ebook) | ISBN 9780717808847 (paperback) | ISBN 9780717808854 (epub)
Subjects: LCSH: Tiago, Manuel—Translations into English. | LCGFT: Short stories.
Classification: LCC PQ9282.I23 P7413 2021 (print) | LCC PQ9282.I23 (ebook) | DDC 869.3/42—dc23
LC record available at https://lccn.loc.gov/2021039636
LC ebook record available at https://lccn.loc.gov/2021039637

ISBN-10: 0-7178-0884-X   ISBN-13: 978-0-7178-0884-7
Typeset by Amnet Systems, Chennai, India

Table of Contents

Frontispiece
Foreword ix
The Slackers 3
Hand in Hand 29
Parallel Stories 43
Délinha 95
Lives 101
A short biographical note on the author 125
About the Translator 127
Questions to Ponder and Discuss 129

The Slackers
and Other Stories

by Manuel Tiago
(Álvaro Cunhal)

Translated by
Eric A. Gordon

The Slackers

*

Hand in Hand

*

Parallel Stories

*

Délinha

*

Lives

Also available from International Publishers
in its series of fictional works by Manuel Tiago

Five Days, Five Nights
"devoid of the stilted political speechifying sometimes found in political fiction, the novella manages to capture the complexities, loneliness, and bravery of ordinary people" (*Monthly Review*)

The Six-Pointed Star
"a breathtaking novel of heartbreaking vignettes" (*Culture Matters*)

The 3rd Floor
"exciting and suspenseful…I could not put the book down as I read the four stories, each in one sitting. Each of them is a page-turner." (*People's World*)

Border Crossings
"A work of unique concept and clever prose, richly translated. It's both engaging and eye-opening." (*People's World*)

Foreword

By Eric A. Gordon

WELCOME to the third and final collection of short stories in the Manuel Tiago series—the first is the previously published *The 3rd Floor and Other Stories of the Portuguese Resistance*, and the second is *Border Crossings*. Here Tiago breaks some new ground in his writing.

The title story, "The Slackers," deals humorously with a mixed bag of misfits who are forced to report to a military correctional camp to complete their obligatory service. So far in the series, this is Tiago's only attempt to portray military life, and he does so from the oblique perspective of open as well as passive resistance to conformity. (Later in the series we will present his *Eulalia's House*, which takes place during the brutal Spanish Civil War.) Reinaldo is a professed Communist, and Braga is a natural-born anti-authoritarian, a kind of visceral anarchist. The brass—as is frequent in satirical military stories—are portrayed as pompous, incompetent and deceitful. Most readers will experience a few laugh-out-loud moments in this riotously dark tale.

Yet there is a larger and later story that is implicit but not told here, which is that the resistance to fascism took place at all levels and in almost every corner of Portuguese society, including in the military itself. Even career officers were eventually convinced that the colonial wars the régime was fighting in Angola, Mozambique and Guinea-Bissau were costly in terms of lives and materiel, and ultimately futile. Besides which, the Communist Party had also made inroads into the military ranks, which made the end-days of the régime that much more of a shock to the system as it was the military itself that sparked the Revolution.

As in several of his other works of fiction, Tiago based his tale on his own life—that is, Álvaro Cunhal's. For a time, in

ix

late 1939 and early 1940, Cunhal was forced to complete his military service in the Disciplinary Company of Penamacor, a municipality in the district of Castelo Branco in east-central Portugal. Later in life he reencountered some of his mates from that period.

"Hand in Hand" is a teenage love story set against the background of the now post-1974 public flowering of the Communist Party as a significant partner in the democratic reconstruction of the country. We want to root so hard for Célia and Luís and hope they make it despite a major obstacle placed in their path.

What we cannot help noticing is that there is no religious moralizing about their relationship—obviously not from the Communist author, but not even from their friends or relations. Portugal was for centuries a Catholic stronghold. Our Lady of Fátima became a Portuguese and worldwide figure of religious and reactionary veneration after her "miraculous" appearance in 1917 with specific warnings about Russia (it was the year of the Bolshevik Revolution). The fascists in power from the 1920s to the 1970s made sure that the Church had a high and privileged status. But its power fell precipitously after the Revolution, especially among youth, who seemed to instinctively adopt principles of free love that freethinkers of all stripes had advocated for at least a century.

The author in this story also calls upon his own memories, having served as a very young man, in his early twenties, as leader of the Federation of Portuguese Communist Youth.

"Parallel Stories" is the centerpiece of the collection, the longest and most developed story in this volume, essentially a novella. At first, the title sounds a bit abstract. But after the main storyline is delineated, it comes into clearer focus. Set, again, in more contemporary democratic times, we see a small regional Communist Party organization (or what would be called a "club" in modern U.S. parlance) struggling with its past as primarily a party of the working class at a time when the working class itself was undergoing profound changes. And in this rural district, the people most motivated to advance ideologically turn out not to be factory workers but agricultural workers and small farmers, with whom the

Party has little experience. In the heat of the "battle of ideas," some people will fall to the wayside while others emerge as new leaders and activists comfortably relating to population groups not ordinarily seen around Party circles.

In the present collection, this story possibly comes closest to the Socialist Realist esthetic, but the author creatively applies it to disagreements and conflicts within the Party itself. While some Communists are portrayed as people stuck in the language, style and prejudices of decades of past practice, others come across as searching, open, compassionate human beings willing to stick their necks out and try new approaches even if they might fail.

The reader will meet some finely drawn characters in this story, which ends with the requisite Socialist Realist optimism.

"Délinha" is also a literary stretch for Manuel Tiago, which many readers might find challenging—not that it's written in an experimental vein as such, but owing to its terrifying Edgar Allan Poe-like persistency of effect. There may be more to the story under the surface, but readers will have to tease that out for themselves.

The final story, "Lives," reads like the précis or treatment of an epic-long family saga à la Charles Dickens, or even a sprawling multi-season TV miniseries. Its time-frame is deliberately obscure, although to be sure, there is an automobile that plays a small part toward the end. Otherwise, we seem to hover anywhere between the late 19th century all the way up through the mid-20th. Society appears fossilized in the ways and manners of bygone times, when the poor rarely strayed far from their "*terra*," their birthplaces. To visit a close relative not so many kilometers away was a rare, cherished event. Even for the dour rural oligarchy there seemed to be little interest in travel, culture, reading, anything that might expand the mind beyond the daily routines at home. It was a desolate, socially regimented system of rigid class distinctions and orders where custom was not casually breached.

The range of social classes, ages and professions of his characters as well as locales of the action—even at one point taking us to Portugal's African colony of Angola—makes this collection a well-rounded portrait of a society before, during and after momentous historic transformations.

Once again, I express my profound indebtedness to those who helped in various aspects of this work: Bill Gregory, Francisco Melo, Gary Bono, Janice Rothstein, John Mueter, José Oliveira, Rich Eisbrouch and the late lamented Steve Johnson.

The Slackers

The Slackers

The Disciplinary Company

"ATTENTION! Right face!" The voice echoed across the parade ground one cold, harsh morning.

It was odd. On the parade ground giving instruction were a captain, a lieutenant, a first sergeant, a second sergeant and two corporals, but there were only eight soldiers.

Once again the commander's voice rang out. "Attention!" followed by the sound of soldiers clicking the heels of their boots. "At ease!"

And so the Disciplinary Company was launched.

The following events all took place during the first months after the Company was established. In ensuing years considerably more soldiers were integrated into the Disciplinary Company—justifying the name "company."

The Company was created so that soldiers from various units could repeat their military service there, having been accused of many offenses—political activities, desertion, theft, brawling and serious breaches of discipline.

As you can see, the inauguration was not illustrious, with just eight correctional soldiers. Eight "correctives"—or slackers, as they came to be known.

Coming from diverse military units, none of them knew anything about the others. Over the first few days they got to know one another. One after the other, they learned why they had been sent there.

Reinaldo

There was a lot of curiosity about Reinaldo.

"Hey, pal, you shave and you brush your teeth every day and always go around so well dressed. So, let's have it—who are you?"

Reinaldo didn't play coy or hard to get. He was the first to allow his companions to get to know him. He had been convicted in a Special Military Court with all the ridiculous pomp and display that made it seem more like a farce than a court of law. The sentence had already been determined by the PIDE, the International and State Defense Police. The judges, high officers all dressed up like characters in a play, unsheathed their swords and solemnly declaimed, as if it were really they who had decided whatever it was, "Oyez! Oyez! The sentence will be read!"

"Wait a minute!" someone interrupted him. "Are you making this up or is that how it really was?"

"It's true, it's the whole truth," Reinaldo affirmed.

After his sentence was over at the Fort of Caxias, he presented himself at the barracks of Infantry 1 ready to do his service, because before he was taken prisoner that's where he'd been assigned and inducted. He had been there only two days when a lieutenant approached him, shouting at him as if he were some lowly loafer.

"The Commander has ordered me to state he does not want you here at this installation any more time than it takes to dispatch you to somewhere else. We don't want people like you here. You are going straight to a Disciplinary Company which has just been created."

"But why were you convicted anyway?"

"I was a member of a Communist Party group."
"You a Communist? You must be joking."
"Yes, a Communist. That's what I am. That's why they sent me here."
"What do you say, boys, is this guy a liar or what?"
"And what did you do before you were taken prisoner? Factory worker, office employee, or—"
"No," Reinaldo responded calmly. "I'm an engineer."
"That's a good one," they said. "Now you're really trying to put one over on us." "Don't lie to us."
"Not at all," Reinaldo insisted. "It's the truth, I'm an engineer—"
He would have continued, but he was called to see the Captain.

The Library

The Captain received him not with his usual gruff voice, but in a moderated and even respectful tone. Also contrary to custom with the other soldiers, he spoke to him not degradingly but in the proper form of address.

He said what he wanted to say in but a few words. He didn't like seeing Reinaldo emptying latrines, scrubbing floors, and tearing weeds out of the parade grounds. In short, he didn't want him to spend his whole day working at the dirtiest jobs with thieves, deserters and vagrants.

"So that's why I want to give you some other work."

Standing at attention, Reinaldo gave no sign of reaction whatsoever.

"We have a library here. They sent it to us, I don't know from where or why. And I'm going to give you work in that library."

He explained his project. The books were all mixed up. The job was to arrange them and make index cards for all of them in alphabetical order, with reference to their respective contents.

"You can take your time with this. You can spend the two years you have to serve here in the library."

Reinaldo grasped the objective of this decision. With the exception of the obligatory sleeping in the barracks and eating in common in the mess hall, it was to completely separate him from the other men sentenced to fulfill their military obligation in the Company.

"So?" the Commander asked.

"Nothing, Captain," Reinaldo answered, still standing at attention. "I will comply with your orders. I will make the index cards just as you have told me."

"Isn't there anything else you'd like to say?" Evidently he was expecting some thanks.

"Yes, Captain. As soon as I have finished the work, I will come and let you know."

The library was a good bunch of books. But arranging them on the shelves and making index cards for each title was an easy chore that did not require much time.

Three days later, he went to the Captain to say that the work was done.

"Done already? You haven't understood me! You could have taken a week or a month, and avoided going back to those worthless slackers."

Reinaldo didn't respond.

"All right," the Captain said, now visibly irritated. "Keep in mind everything I just told you. Now make me an index card file of the chapter titles in every book. Do you get it?"

"Yes, I get everything perfectly, Captain."

And as Reinaldo was leaving the room the Captain added, "Think hard about everything I told you and be careful. It would be best if you understood and complied. Don't create more troubles for yourself than the ones you already have."

Reinaldo threw himself into the work in a frenzy. In less than a month he reappeared with the finished job.

The Captain received him, infuriated. "Stand at attention!"

"I have been since I entered," Reinaldo answered.

The Captain pounded his desk. "If you feel fine with those slackers, then dammit go back to them. You'll become one of them in every way. But don't ever count on me for anything more. Stand at attention and listen."

"Since I came into your office I've always been standing at attention," Reinaldo repeated.

"Shut up, you insolent slacker!" the Captain bellowed. "And get out of my sight!"

In the Barracks

The barracks consisted of a wide, poorly lit space. Dozens of beds were set out in two rows with an aisle down the middle, foot opposite foot. The first eight beds were occupied by the first eight slacker soldiers who inaugurated the Company with the goal of completing or repeating their military service.
That night they continued recounting their stories.
It was half in jest and half in seriousness that Varino spoke of himself.

"I've been like this since I was a kid. There was always the temptation and the thrill. If something caught my attention, *whht!* I'd steal it. It could be fruit in a grocery shop, a few banknotes, bags unattended on a countertop. Whatever came into the net was fish. I especially enjoyed the mule game. You know what the mule game is? It's really fun. You buy something and you show a large banknote to pay for it. The vendor prepares your change and the merchandise. And you, *whisshh!* That's where the thrill comes in. Without handing over the banknote you showed, you pick up the merchandise and your change, turn around and walk out with the most natural innocence. By the time the guy realizes his mistake, you're nowhere to be found."

"Did it always work out that well for you?" they asked.

"Yes and no," Varino went on. "One day—I was enlisted by then—I fell upon a great stroke of luck. Imagine this: I go to clean the officers' washroom and what do I see? Next to the washbasin there's a shiny watch. And what a watch it was! All gold. The hands gold, the case gold, and the band gold. Gold in plain sight. So think about it, guys. If it was left there, not even God would punish me for taking it—a gold watch on my wrist to show my buddies."

"And didn't the officer notice it was missing?" asked Zé.

"That I don't know. I do know they saw it on my wrist and everything followed from that—a year in jail and orders to report for service here in the Company."

Next to speak, César didn't elaborate. He was enlisted in an infantry unit, but he couldn't bear it. The officers treated the soldiers worse than dogs, and he wasn't going to put up with it.

"Worse than dogs? What do you mean by that?" one of the companions asked.

It was stupid orders, insults, punishment. He for one had had enough of that, and one day, during a break, he left the base intending not to return. But he was an ass for returning to his family home. Two days later, a patrol from the base came and arrested him. He was tried and sentenced, and when he got out of prison he presented himself at the base.

"It's good you showed up," an officer told him. "You're no use doing your service here. You're going straight to the Disciplinary Company that's just been established." And that's all César could tell.

Zé wanted to go next. "Like Reinaldo, I too, my friends, am political. In the military I didn't hide it. I spoke badly of the government, I spoke badly of the priests, badly of the rich and—this was my first mistake—I spoke badly of the military."

Everyone wanted to know, "Who did you say it to?"

"Naturally, only to the other soldiers. But besides the soldiers, there was a sergeant there who was great. He was always saying how everything was wrong—the food, the uniforms, the discipline. So I believed the sergeant thought like me. I sought him out and I told him everything I was saying to the other soldiers. Bad against the government, bad against the priests, bad against the rich, and bad against the military service. The guy heard me out, and at the end he shouted, 'Are you an idiot or what? From this moment on you are apprehended, I'm telling the Commander and putting you in the brig.' I was in a cell for two weeks."

"And then?" someone asked, impatiently.

"Then they took me out of my cell, ripped the patches off my uniform, and ordered me to present myself here at the Disciplinary Company."

"And how about you, Berto? Aren't you talking?"

Aside from being a troublemaker, Berto enjoyed joking and making fun. He invented such fitting names for officers and sergeants that, in the soldiers' slang, they started referring to them that way. One captain had a thunderous voice, but he always gave nonsensical instructions. He came to be known as Dunder. A lieutenant who noticed anything out of place and scolded the solider for it, wound up being the Nitpick. An arrogant, bossy sergeant became the Rain Commander.

Everyone spoke that way. If they knew the captain would be giving instructions that day, they started saying, "Dunder's on duty today."

It was the same with the others. "Did you see? Nitpick shined his shoes."

"Careful with the Rain Commander, he's always looking to punish someone."

"And they never caught you? You were never punished?"

"One day the sergeant heard someone say, 'Careful, here comes the Rain Commander.' The sergeant was touchy," Berto said. "'Soldiers have a name and a number,' the sergeant warned. 'Who are you calling Rain Commander?' It's that guy over there, sergeant—'

"'We do not accept nicknames here,' the sergeant shouted. 'One of these days one of you guys is going to the brig.'"

Reinaldo remembered to ask, "But in the end why did they send you here?"

"Since you ask, here goes." And Berto bragged about his adventures. On his free time he'd visit the whores in the alleys around the Cais do Sodré port.

"Did you have a lot of them?"

"I don't want to exaggerate, but every night I fucked three or four."

The pimps didn't appreciate the competition, so they got together and attacked him with razors in their fists, and he returned to the base majorly messed up.

"Meaning, they did a big number on you."

"They did, but I gave them back more than they gave me," Berto continued. "I didn't give up. I went back to the Cais do Sodré and from there things went from bad to worse. They beat me up again, and I showed up at the base with my uniform all torn. That was all it took. They gave me my marching orders to come here."

"There are no Cais do Sodré whores here, pal. Only if you can manage to seduce some girl somehow."

"We'll see," Berto replied. "You gave me a good idea."

"And you, Afonso, you came here and right away they started you off as a cook, but now you're here with us in the barracks. So who are you, really? And why did you come here?"

"I don't know," Afonso answered, and refused to provide any further explanation.

Braga

Only Braga and Licas had not yet spoken about their cases.

Braga's case was most special. He was a heavy-set man, older than the rest of the Company. They asked him what regiment he had come from.

"From carrying water barrels at the Fort of Elvas," he answered.

Then he told his story. He had been soldier no. 164 of the 2nd Artillery Battery 2. He obeyed orders, but that didn't stop his superiors from stepping on his corns. There was a lieutenant there who liked to humiliate the soldiers, and Braga could not reconcile himself to that. On the training field, the lieutenant gave preposterous instructions just to amuse himself, turning his soldiers into puppets.

"One, two! One, two! One, two! About-face! Back! Attention! At ease! Attention! At ease! Attention!"

Braga was not one to put up with it. So, if the lieutenant wanted to play with the soldiers, it popped into Braga's head he could play with the lieutenant. And he did.

"Attention!" the lieutenant barked. And Braga assumed the position of at ease.

"Hey, you! Are you a simpleton or what? *Attention!*" the lieutenant repeated. Braga made an about-face and resumed his position of at ease.

The lieutenant became furious and, fisting his billyclub, shouted in Braga's face, "Either you stand at attention or I'm going to bust your snout."

Braga stood there indifferent, and the lieutenant wielded his club, whacking him repeatedly on the face.

With his face all bloodied, Braga tried to defend himself. Not even he could explain the temptation that overcame him. In one quick movement he socked the lieutenant hard, making him fall to the ground with his legs in the air.

The lieutenant rose to his feet, grabbed his pistol and pointed it directly at Braga's chest. Braga saw his eyes full of hate, the man barely containing his intention to shoot and kill him.

The sergeant and other soldiers ran toward them, took hold of the lieutenant and helped him pull himself together and leave the parade ground. Others took Braga away.

He paid a heavy price: Four years in military prison, then two more carrying water barrels at the Fort of Elvas, subjected to a constant barrage of provocations and bad treatment.

And now that he was free once again, he'd been sent to Disciplinary Company to redo his training. No, no way. He wouldn't be able to take it.

"Don't say that. Time passes fast here. You can see we're all good people. We even have an engineer among us, what more do you want?"

"Uh-uh, fellas. I can't take this and I have to think about how I'm gonna get out of here."

"You just have to leave. One day, when we go into town, just go off and desert," said one.

No. Desert, no. He'd be apprehended again and put in jail. He had to think of something better.

Licas

"And you, Licas? You're always chiming in, but we haven't heard a word from you today. What do you have to say?"

Licas began telling his story. "My dad wasn't a bad guy. Only sometimes, after he'd had a few. A good guy. But when he was in the mood for beating me, I'd go flying to the ceiling. I played marbles and copped some from the other kids. Anyway, my dad came home one day in a particularly foul mood, I don't know why. He didn't tell me anything. He took the box I kept my marbles in and threw them all out. I had more than a hundred. We lived on Fountain Street, a very steep street. The old man went to the window and tossed them all. You should have seen it! Licas watched from another window, crushed and full of rage seeing his beautiful marbles bouncing around on the sidewalk and rolling down the street. And the other boys laughing, shouting, running to grab my wonderful marbles. Licas was speechless and trembling. The old man threw the last marble, slowly closed the window and went in. And me, I stayed by my window a very long time looking out at the street and wanting to cry. At dinner that night, I was silent. I looked over at my dad, I looked at my aunt, and said nothing. But at last I couldn't hold it in. I turned to the old man and said, 'Dad...a little while ago...you didn't have the right—'

"The old guy raised his eyes and placed his spoon on his plate. He gave me one sideways look and *pow!* I can't even tell you. What a big blow Licas got. I couldn't even finish eating.

"You want to know what my life was like? That's what it was, more or less. But one day there was a big event.

"I never knew who my mother was. My dad lived without a wife. So one day he brought a woman back to the house. And I started hating her like you can't imagine. My aunt was a deaf-mute, but very clever. It's true. That other woman began living on the next floor above. One day I turned to my aunt and I did like this: I pointed up to the ceiling. Then I pretended to curl my mustache like my dad would do. Then I put my right hand on top of my left hand and twisted my fingers. I can't tell you any more. That night the woman came down. And my aunt grabbed a knife and attacked her. She defended herself but instead of grabbing my aunt's arm or hand, she grabbed the blade by the sharpened edge and wound up with the palm of her hand cut to the bone. There was quite a hullabaloo in the house that night—the woman moaning with her hands wrapped up in old rags, and my aunt receiving such a beating that she stayed in bed for two weeks unable to get up.

"Besides being violent, my old man was really stupid. Because the more he beat, the more troubles he got into.

"One day, the woman said I was becoming quite the clever lad. And you know why? The sewing machine had been moved upstairs, and she wanted my aunt to go up and help her. All this by gestures, understand, because as I told you, my aunt was a deaf-mute. She misunderstood the signs. She thought she was going out to the street and she put her little hat on. Then the woman said, 'Where does that old lady think she's going, and with that little hat?' And I said she had no right to make fun of my aunt. And she turned to me and said again that I was becoming quite the clever lad. I didn't answer her and she got more and more exasperated. She went on shouting and I stayed silent. Finally she lost all patience, and was yelling and flailing around so much that she fell on the floor and I can't even tell you! She wound up on the floor with her legs in the air. How happy I was to see her like that with her legs up!

"Just to be on the cautious side, I asked my aunt for an early dinner so I could go out to the street and watch out for my old man to see if I could tell if he was in a good or a bad mood. Only later I went inside the house. I pushed the door open with trepidation, expecting that right away my dad would land a bunch of punches on me. You can imagine how Licas was shaking, like a leaf. But the old man just sat down and hardly moved. I was on the verge of trying to sneak into my room when he looked at me and said, 'Come here.' And I stood in front of him and braced myself. You should have seen Licas waiting there for a while with his heart racing so hard it was like a horse. Finally the old guy looked at me and said straight out, 'From today on, that woman will serve as your mother.' He repeated, 'that woman.' I didn't say anything and went to bed. My dad didn't say any more. From that day on I had a stepmother."

Licas now had the eyes of someone lost in the night recalling such sad memories. Then he went on.

"One day I almost died drowning. I used to go fishing off the pier. I spent hour after hour there. Sometimes I gave the fish away, other times I sold it to the fishwives. I didn't want it for myself, not even to take back home, because almost always it was shad, and shad is all bones. Not even cats like it.

"But one time I wasn't paying attention, and I don't know how it happened but there was Licas standing in the river. What saved me is that the water there wasn't very deep. It was about two meters and I hit the bottom with my feet and came back up to breathe. You should have seen Licas practically being dragged under. And what got me so angry was on the pier there was a guy who barely moved a finger. He watched me and just sat there perfectly calm, like he was at the theater. I was just about done for with all the water I was taking in, until a boat came along loaded with sardines, and the fishermen lifted me up and I stretched out half dead on top of the fish, drenched to my bones. My old man was surely going to give me a good thrashing. When we landed, I headed home, trembling like a leaf, cold and afraid. The fish scales had stuck to my clothing. I was walking all shining with silver scales and the people passing saw me and laughed at me. My dad was gonna beat me good, I knew it.

"But no. When I got home, he looked at me and asked, 'What happened?' I explained, 'I almost died drowning.' I can't even tell you. I never saw my old man laugh so hard in my life. He looked at me shining with sardine scales attached to my clothes and he laughed like he was insane. And that surprised me so much, and I was so nervous, that I broke out laughing too."

"You've gone and told us your whole life, Licas," Berto interrupted. "But you still haven't said how come they sent you here."

"I was just going to say. One night, at bedtime at the base where I was doing my service, 37 came to talk to me. 'Listen, Licas, my friend.' A kindly sergeant had warned him that that night they were going to make an inspection. 'Listen, Licas, I have a wallet with me that I stole. I'm asking you to hold it for me while they do the search.' Now, Licas had never stolen anything, but after all, you do a favor for your friends. I hid the wallet, they searched 37 and didn't find anything. And me hiding the wallet in my pocket. 'Thanks, pal,' 37 said to me when the search was over, 'give me the wallet.' 'Don't even think about it, 37,' I told him. 'I don't collaborate in thievery from other people.' He threatened me, but I knew a thing or two about punches and I didn't hand him the wallet. The next morning I went looking for the kindly sergeant. 'Sergeant, sir, I found this wallet on the ground.' 'Hmm! Now you want to save your ass, but you don't fool me, you rat.' I explained that I had simply found the wallet. But they doubted my word and believed I was in on the game, and gave me orders to report here."

"You're a fool, Licas," Varino said. "You could have kept the dough. 37 couldn't snitch on you."

"That's the way I am, what do you want?" Licas answered. "I had the life I had. But I never stole anything from anyone."

Braga Goes to the Hospital

"You just got here and you want to get out already? That's shameful, Braga. The people here are really nice. You'll spend a quiet two years with us like a vacation, and then you'll get on with your life just fine." Varino made fun of Braga because he kept saying over and over again that he wanted to be finally free to get on with his life.

If Varino and Licas kidded him gently, Reinaldo spoke seriously to Braga. "I only see one way, Braga. You have to go to the Medical Board for them to decide you're unfit for service. But how will you get to the Medical Board? And if you do, such a decision is far from certain. You must have health issues to warrant it."

Braga thought and thought, and came to a decision. It was risky. It could put an end to his health forever, but it was better to try everything before submitting to staying there two years.

His plan was to drink a concoction with petroleum. His companions would sound the alarm and he would be taken to the hospital. Given his condition, he'd be referred to the Board, hoping he'd be free of the military forever. He was prepared to do it, but he needed help from his companions.

"Don't count on me for this," said Reinaldo. "What you want to do would be the end of you. It's crazy. If you carry this idea forward, I can say for my part, I knew nothing about it."

Licas and Varino, on the contrary, offered to help him. "Yeah, you're crazy, that's true. But since you're being a mule about it, we all see you're going ahead with it anyway. So just tell us how we can help you."

Then Braga explained his plan in detail. It would be late at night, after the silence bell had rung, when no one from the Company would be returning to the barracks. He would drink the potion, lie down, and cover himself completely with a sheet. The companions would stay on watch and only call for help when he said to.

"Count on me," Licas said.

"Me too," Varino seconded. No one else offered to help.

They chose a day when first sergeant Serafim would be on duty. He was a good man and, once alerted, would order that Braga be taken to the town health center to get his stomach pumped and then later go to the military hospital.

Once again Reinaldo attempted to dissuade him from this idea. "It's almost suicide."

But Braga had decided, and nothing would stop him.

The act had a certain solemnity to it. Braga imbibed the drink, moaned with the heat it produced, lay down quickly on his bed and covered himself from head to toe with a sheet.

Except for Licas and Varino, the other soldiers sat on their beds in nervous silence.

"Do you hear me?" Licas asked above the sheet.

"Yes," Braga answered in a quietly whining voice.

"As soon as you say, we'll call for help," said Varino.

Unlike all the others, quiet and uneasy, Licas and Varino didn't stop talking.

"Licas is here, my friend. I'm not going anywhere, make sure you don't go anywhere either. It would be a shame, us here waiting for you and you already gone."

"Listen, we're waiting for you to say the word to call for help. Don't just lie there not talking and upsetting us."

Time passed and Braga still didn't ask for help.

"He's gonna die there," came an unexpected voice from the barracks, where all until now had been silent except for Licas and Varino.

"You better call for help already," said another voice.

"Shhhh!" Licas told them. "The man knows what he's doing and what he wants."

But Licas and Varino were getting nervous too. They increased their pace of asking, "Not yet? Not yet?" above the sheet.

"Hey, buddy! This guy is a real hero!" Varino exclaimed.

"Now?" they asked again.

Finally, Braga's body shifted under the sheet, and it was a supplicating voice that answered, "Now!"

Like a rocket, Licas left the barracks sprinting. The help did not come, and in place of the earlier silence, now Braga's groans could be heard.

It was some time before Licas reappeared, suddenly and out of breath.

Though his absence was strictly forbidden, first sergeant Serafim was not on the base. But the head nurse would come with a stretcher.

By now Braga was groaning constantly.

"They're coming, they're coming!" Varino and Licas reassured him.

It took so long, but eventually the nurse arrived. They pulled Braga out of bed and laid him down on the stretcher, covering him with the sheet.

"Two to take him with me!" the nurse shouted.

It wasn't necessary to ask. Licas and Varino lifted the stretcher to take Braga away. They left the barracks as quickly as they could.

Those who hadn't said anything throughout this whole scene then started talking. They remained together a few more minutes, as if expecting news. But no news came, and who could tell how many more hours they'd have to wait before the two friends returned from the health center?

They turned off the light. The barracks descended into darkness.

Calomel

Everybody knew that first sergeant Serafim was an incorrigible alcoholic. His wife and son too.

For having been absent from the base that night while on duty, he was called to the captain, who upbraided him with the severity of his dereliction.

"I was feeling very sick," Serafim tried to justify himself. "I went home to take some medicine."

"You're making that up, sergeant. If you wanted some medicine we had the head nurse here at the base who was on duty."

"I didn't remember that," the sergeant clumsily tried to defend himself.

"Very well, sergeant. If you are sick, our doctor will examine you and prescribe the necessary medicine."

The doctor saw him. Serafim was still reeking of alcohol.

"What's your problem?"

"Dizziness and vomiting, doctor."

"I'm going to prescribe a remedy for you. Return home and take the indicated dose two times."

The sergeant went home, and the doctor went to speak with the captain. "Since he said he was absent from the base because he was sick, now he'll be convinced he is. I'm giving him calomel. It's a purgative. He'll be defecating day and night. It can be dangerous, but I prescribed the right dose."

"Dangerous?"

"Yes, dangerous, because if the dose is excessive it's poisonous. But I expect everything will go well."

"If that's your judgment, go ahead," the captain agreed.

Serafim went home and, not being required to be on duty, had his drinks as usual. Following the doctor's instruction, he took the calomel purgative that was sent over from the base. Twenty-four hours later he was dead.

"You gave him too big a dose," the captain remarked.

"The dose was correct. But I didn't count on him getting drunk."

"Grave negligence, doctor."

"What can be done? It was a miscalculation."

"We cannot tell this to anyone, doctor."

"Naturally, captain."

The task now was to no longer think about the crime committed and organize the funeral.

The Vigil

With the first sergeant dead, the second sergeant, a blowhard of the first order, assumed his duties. Whatever Serafim had that was gentle and accommodating, Garruncho was an authoritarian. He had his men line up on the parade ground to give them orders. The corrective soldiers, now seven since Braga had gone to the hospital, would all spend the night doing vigil service over the body of the deceased.

Remaining on duty at the base were the lieutenant Martins and sergeant Garruncho, plus the two corporals.

The correctives would serve not in shirtsleeves, as they went about their usual duty, but in full uniform.

"Uniformed, sergeant, sir?" Licas asked. "Without a sash, and with no insignia of the Company on our collars and birettas?"

Having difficulty responding, the sergeant finally made his decision. "I can get hold of three or four sashes, but so far I don't have insignias for the Company."

"Some service!" Licas exclaimed. "We'll present quite a figure. It'll be the Company's dishonor."

The sergeant insisted. All he could get were the three or four sashes, but in compensation he would get white gloves for everyone.

Licas broke out laughing. "I couldn't help myself, sergeant, sir! And you, our commander, you'll also have white gloves without a sash or insignias of the Company?"

The sergeant had already decided what he was going to wear. He'd go in his old uniform as an infantry sergeant, which is what he was before being sent here. But the fact is that being in command of a group of maladroits would not reflect well on him, crossing through town at the head of a military force. He needed to see what else he could do.

He did manage to get sashes for everyone. Freshly shaved, their uniforms ironed, they marched that night to the vigil at the dead man's house.

Serafim was quite tall, and his coffin occupied much of the space in the improvised mourning chamber. Seated at the head, the widow appeared to be soaked in alcohol. Her lamentations rose up in great weeping.

"Look at this. Such a small coffin for my husband. He barely fits it, poor thing. Look at this, just look."

Six soldiers stood at attention, three on each side of the coffin. Despite their tacky uniforms, their respectful demeanor lent the proper military dignity. The seventh sat on a chair, ready to relieve one of the six.

So they passed a good part of the night, silently, standing at attention, and watching the coffin. To their surprise, the body moved. The stomach expanded and deflated. They didn't know that was the effect of the calomel purgative the doctor had ordered that had poisoned him.

The widow didn't cease crying. The night would have continued like that if not for the arrival of the deceased's son, also visibly inebriated. He went up to the soldiers and in a subdued voice told them, "Hey, boys! Why don't you come inside and have a glass and eat something? We're all in there drinking to my father's soul. Three of you can come, then the other three."

The soldiers paid him no mind. But as soon as he had left, an old lady coming from the next room came to speak to them.

"Sons, it's very cold here. You can't stay here like this all night. Come with me. In the next room it's warmer."

What to do? The widow had already gotten up and left with her son. To remain there at attention didn't make sense. They accompanied the old woman to the next room.

Two other aged women, dressed in black, were seated around a portable heater. "There's some chairs over there, have a seat, sons," said the old lady who had brought them in. "Aunt Brígida," she said, pointing to one of the other women, "is relating what happened to her."

"It was a jinx at the cross in the cemetery by the road to the mills. Surely Serafim passed by there one night and was cursed. I passed by there one night myself. When I got to the cross I heard a voice."

And, imitating a deep, scary voice, old Brígida continued: "'*Whoo goes theere?*' Ay, children, I was shaking from head to foot. A suffering soul appeared before me. God make me blind if it's not the truth."

Turning to the soldiers, she gave them her advice: "You should never go at night along the road to the mills. I wasn't hexed. But Serafim didn't escape."

Very seriously, Varino asked, "Listen, Senhora Brígida, what was the suffering soul like?"

"It was like this, very tall, wrapped in a white sheet. It must have left the cemetery to hover around the area."

"What idiocy," Afonso whispered into Reinaldo's ear, almost inaudibly.

One of the old ladies heard his remark clearly. "If you don't believe it," she said, "I'll denounce you as an apostate. Listening to you is almost like hearing the voice of the Devil himself."

"It's completely true what Senhora Brígida is saying," one of the other old women added. "I can confirm it myself. I also passed by there one night and I also saw a suffering soul. It was exactly like Senhora Brígida said. I ran away as fast as I could and escaped the curse."

By this time Licas couldn't resist entering the conversation. "Speaking for myself, I believe everything you ladies are saying. I also had an encounter with a suffering soul."

"See? See? There's one of your own saying it's true."

"It was back where I come from," Licas continued. "It was night, and I passed in front of a cross dedicated to Saint Ildefonso. As I passed, the suffering soul rose up on my path. 'Stop there, oh mortal man. Stop there!' You should have seen Licas! This Licas has no fear. I was carrying a club in my hand and *pow! pow!* I finished him off."

"And then?" the old ladies asked.

"Licas escaped the jinx. And that's why I'm here with you, ready for the next one."

And so passed the night. In the morning the exhausted soldiers returned to the base to prepare for the funeral.

At the Base

As the vigil for Sergeant Serafim was proceeding in his house, back at the base another important meeting was taking place with the captain in his office. Lieutenant Martins was present, as well as Second Sergeant Garruncho, the Company doctor, and the nurse, Corporal José Relvas—a true council of the general staff.

The subject was nothing more nor less than making decisions about the funeral the next day. One idea was that as the coffin was lowered into the earth, the soldiers would fire off a salute.

"Bullets? Don't even think about it," the captain pronounced.

"We have rubber bullets," the lieutenant observed.

"Not that either," the captain refused. "The slackers are dangerous people. Someone could misdirect their aim."

A nervous shiver coursed through the office.

Out of this indecisive impasse, the nurse corporal brought up an unexpected idea based on an experience he had had. Namely that, in place of metal bullets or rubber bullets, they place in the cartridge plugs of cotton specially prepared for the effect.

"Nonsense!" the captain interrupted.

"Ridiculous!" the lieutenant added.

The corporal did not give up. If they would permit, he would tell them about his experience.

"Let him speak, captain," the doctor offered. "It will be amusing to hear it, I'm sure."

"Go ahead," the captain said.

Relvas did not need any further encouragement.

As a boy he had been a hunter. He and his friends used to go out in a group after rabbits. In the group there was one who considered himself better than the rest. We needed to puncture his balloon. He, Relvas, had an idea. Load his rifle with shot made of cotton wads.

"You're kidding," the doctor laughed.

No, no, he wasn't lying. That's what they did. He himself managed to load the braggart's rifle. The group went out to hunt. *Boom, boom, boom!* rang out shots from one and another, and several rabbits were killed. At the end, the big-shot was desolate and disturbed, not knowing what had happened.

"I must be sick, guys. The rabbits jumped right out from under my feet, I aimed, *boom, boom*, and they hopped away right out into the field."

"We can accept the idea, but if you're trying to deceive us," the captain concluded, "you will pay dearly for your little joke."

The corporal offered to prepare the cotton bullets that night and place them in the rifles the slackers would take to the funeral.

The others should let him spend the night in the armory, and the following morning all would be ready according to plan.

"Proceed!" the captain ordered, rising from his chair, though personally with scant confidence in the order he had just given.

The Funeral

The funeral for First Sergeant Serafim was a major event in the area. The people had never before attended and participated in a military funeral. Also for the first time, the people witnessed an armed contingent of correctives from the Disciplinary Company marching through the streets.

It was a grand day for Second Sergeant Garruncho. He retrieved his old uniform smelling of mothballs from his trunk and there he'd be, back in his home territory, commanding a military force.

The soldiers marched three on one side of the funeral carriage, three on the other. It's true they wore strange uniforms and mismatched caps with no military insignias whatsoever. But the earnest way they paraded, guns on their shoulders, made anyone forget those deficiencies and demanded genuine respect.

It was inexplicable why Afonso, the cook, had been ordered to remain with the soldiers keeping guard at the base during the funeral. The way he was treated continued to be a mystery.

Behind the funeral carriage followed the grieving family of the deceased and a big throng of penitent folk in the cortege.

The attendance was even bigger at the cemetery. Word had spread that there was to be an honor salute as the coffin descended into the grave. People's curiosity was heightened, and the ambiance was more festive than funereal.

The coffin was removed from the carriage and taken to the gravesite. Second Sergeant Garruncho's anxiously awaited great moment had arrived.

He ordered his platoon into formation. The coffin was lowered into the ground, and the sergeant shouted, "Present arms! Prepare fire!"

Trrch, trrch, trrch sounded the rifles, the cylinder heads pulled back, bullets in their chambers. Some in the crowd covered their ears.

"Fire!" the sergeant thundered.

Pfssh, pfssh, pfssh. Softly and discreetly resounded the wads of cotton the corporal nurse had contrived.

Reinaldo Makes a Decision

That week no one talked about anything else. The most popular opinion was that the slackers had set up a subterfuge. Some people, however, discredited that version.

During that time Reinaldo came to a decision. He was definitely not prepared to spend two years there in the Company. Besides which, his comrades in Lisbon had written saying how much they needed him.

The idea emerged gradually. He recalled that a while back he had a strong pain in his abdomen, and the diagnosis was chronic appendicitis.

He remembered, too, the doctors telling him that if he had intense pain pressing on a certain point in his abdomen, it could be acute appendicitis, warranting immediate surgical intervention. He committed that point to memory, below the bellybutton and three or four fingers to the right.

So that was his plan: To simulate an attack of acute appendicitis and be sent to a military hospital, then get the Medical Board to declare him unfit for military service.

Said and done. One day he stayed behind in the barracks and complained of unbearable pain in his abdomen.

"Could he be pretending?" the captain asked the doctor.

"Let's wait a few days and see," the doctor counseled. "If he stays in bed complaining I'll go see him."

At the barracks Reinaldo did not reveal his plan to his companions. And he refused to eat.

"Reinaldo, Reinaldo, my boy. Don't take us for fools," said Licas. "The way you're going, you're not going to die of sickness, you'll die of hunger."

He continued saying he was hurting a lot and couldn't eat.

One day, the others couldn't wait any longer. Afonso the cook showed up with a cloth-covered dish. "It's for you to eat, Reinaldo."

"No. I've already said so!"

"Don't deceive us, friend," Varino whispered to him. "We don't deserve it."

Temptation won out. Afonso uncovered the dish and who could resist? A steak, a sunny side-up egg, potato fries and bread.

"This is going to make me worse," Reinaldo said, still persisting with his feckless lie. "But I want to honor your good intentions." Biting off and chewing with pleasure, he ate it all and wiped his plate with a piece of bread.

That's how it went for a few more days. Afonso brought him lunch and Reinaldo didn't have to be forced.

"So now, you little lying saint," Varino told him, "your stomach isn't hurting so much and you're gaining strength."

Meanwhile, the captain spoke again with the doctor. "He's still complaining and not eating," the captain told him. "Wouldn't it be best if you went to see him?"

Two days later the doctor visited the barracks. "Undress yourself so I can take a look."

Reinaldo removed his clothes, and the doctor started to press his belly with two fingers. "Here? Does it hurt?"
"No, doctor."
"And here?"
"Not there either. Maybe a little more to the right."
"Here?"
"No, doctor, below the bellybutton, a little more, and over to the right."
"Now? Does it hurt?"
"Press there, doctor." The doctor pressed and Reinaldo let out a scream.
"That hurt a lot, doctor. It's unbearable."
"Okay," the doctor said. "That's it, then. I see what it is." And he went to speak with the captain.
"It's an appendicitis attack. In fact, acute appendicitis."
"And?"
"It's an infallible diagnosis, Captain, sir. Any competent doctor would recognize it. Sharp pain under pressure on that point—the so-called McBurney's point—is an infallible sign of acute appendicitis. It's a definitive diagnosis in 99 percent of cases."
"So now what, doctor?"
"If you don't want him to die here, which would be very bad for the Company, you'd best send him immediately to a military hospital in the district."
In the afternoon there was a jitney going to the nearest railway station. There he would take a train to the district capital.
Supported by his companions who could barely contain their hilarity and were thoroughly enjoying the show, Reinaldo was led to the jitney. That same evening Reinaldo went to the military hospital.
"Get better, buddy!" Varino shouted after him at parting.
"I hope your pain goes away fast, you little trickster!" Licas called out to him.
Over the following weeks, the captain did what he had never done before. At night he visited the barracks to talk things over.
"The doctor decided to send him to the hospital, and he went. He wouldn't have died of pain—he didn't fool me. But since he's so stubborn, he could have died of hunger."

"If you will permit me, Senhor Captain," said Licas, "Reinaldo had already lost his strength. Just drinking water he wouldn't have lasted but a few more days."

On other visits to the barracks the captain spoke in different tones. About Reinaldo and Braga both having gone to the hospital with an eye toward getting declared unfit by the Medical Board. But they shouldn't have any illusions! "They're going to have to return and perform their two-year term of service." Raising his voice even higher, he added, "And I'll be keeping an eye on them, that's for sure."

Return

A communication came from the military hospital that the two sick men the Company had sent them would be appearing at the base the following day.

The captain did not suppress his pleasure. Once again that night he walked to the barracks to share the news.

"Let this be a lesson to you all," he lectured them. "Those two fakers never fooled me. They'll be here tomorrow and I'll be waiting to finally teach them what this Company is all about. They will be made to do their service here for two whole years. I'll show them to watch their step."

The next day, arriving by the jitney, they presented themselves at the guardhouse. The corporal on duty informed the lieutenant, and the two men were escorted to the barracks.

Throughout the base there suddenly arose a thundering racket, with shouts of "*Viva!*," raucous laughter and animated talk such as never before heard on the base.

"Go over there and see what's happening," the captain ordered Sergeant Garruncho. "And make those bums behave themselves."

The sergeant approached with some trepidation. The uproar didn't cease. When the sergeant learned the reason for all the shouting, he felt his blood freezing in his veins. The news was magnificent: Reinaldo and Braga had been discharged by the Medical Board. They were returning to the base now only to collect their things and leave forever.

"Impossible!" the captain bellowed. "Or everything is crazy."

It was true, the sergeant told him. He himself had seen the orders they brought from the hospital. No one saw the captain on the base for many days.

But in the meantime many things happened. Braga and Reinaldo said they didn't have money, and that the Company should give them their tickets and the necessary papers to take the jitney and the train to return to their hometowns.

They got their answer from Sergeant Garruncho. He had express orders from the captain: These two were no longer soldiers. Let them fend for themselves.

Reinaldo and Braga exchanged thoughts. From the Disciplinary Company to the train station was a good ten kilometers. "I'm prepared to walk ten kilometers," Reinaldo said, "but you're still recovering and in pain. Maybe it would be better if we stayed here a few days until I get the money I asked for from Lisbon."

"No," Braga said decisively. "Not one more day on this damn base. And neither should we accept it if our companions want to pitch in for our transportation. We'll just go to the station on foot, the two of us. I'll hold up." Later, on the train, with the help of their release papers from the military hospital, they'd find a way to get home.

The farewell in the barracks was emotional. There was no lack of lamentation—nor of jokes and laughter.

"We're going to miss you," Berto said.

"Long live discharge!" Licas cried.

"Now watch your health, guys, don't get into any more trouble," said Varino with uncommon seriousness.

"And you, Afonso, nothing to say?"

The man of few words, the mysterious Afonso, kept his response simple. "As always, I just take everything in stride."

In the late afternoon, during their off-time, everyone accompanied the two former soldiers now with baggage in their hands.

Some passersby saw them. "And now where are the slackers going, all together like they were marching somewhere?"

"Up to no good, for sure. Maybe we should warn the base."

The slackers continued on their way, crossing through the town until they came to the start of the road. They stood together, almost at attention.

"See you again some day," Braga said.

"I'll never forget you guys," said Reinaldo.

They set out on the road, accompanied by their companions' silent watch.

They were still within view, but as they came to the first bend in the road, they stopped, turned around and waved goodbye.

The others too waved goodbye and remained there a while longer gazing at the road, standing still, each man wordlessly wrapped in his own thoughts.

Hand in Hand

WHAT a beautiful sight—the youth demonstration, with red flags, colorful banners, songs, slogans of the day, struggle, confidence, happiness! Bright hues, sound and movement fill the space. The parade files down the Avenue. Spanning the main thoroughfare, from curb to curb, the young people hand in hand form a cordon marching in front of the sound car. They enthusiastically shout, "Always and now, the youth are at the prow!" "The people united will never be defeated!"

One next to the other, hand in hand in the cordon, a boy and girl stand out for the passion with which they shout the slogans and sing the songs. Full of enthusiasm, they look straight ahead. Only in the middle of the Avenue do they look at one another, and they smile, surprised by what they see. And all the way to Restauradores, they catch a glance at each other every time they call out a slogan, making a harmony of two amidst the larger chorus.

At Restauradores, where the demonstration ends, an orator is giving his speech. The human cordon breaks apart. The two youngsters remain just a moment longer holding hands.

"Hey, you want to meet again?" he asked.

"Sounds good," she answered. "Come by when my school classes let out."

"What school?"

"Pedro Nunes!"

Letting go of her comrade's hand, she raced off to join up with the girlfriends she came with.

* * *

It wasn't easy for the boy to meet up with her. He didn't know what time her classes let out. And since he worked at the military shipyard, he only got off at five.

He ran to the school as soon as he could. The porter told him that classes had ended at four, but there were still some students on the athletic field. He did not allow him to enter, and made him wait, impatiently. Maybe she was among the students who were still there.

He wasn't mistaken. There they came leaving in a group. He met them on their path and took the girl by the arm. "Listen, want to come with me?"

"You?" she asked, bewildered.

"Would you like to take a walk?"

"I can't now, I'm with people."

"Célia!" her friends called out.

"Sunday?"

"Where?"

"Célia!" again her friends called.

"I have to go. Bye."

"Sunday! Here! Three o'clock!" he said as she ran off to join her friends, and disappeared without even a glance back.

* * *

Luís was on time. Sunday at three o'clock he was at the school door. Célia hadn't arrived yet, but soon showed up. She appeared from the edge of the public garden next to the school, walking naturally, neither slow nor in a hurry.

"Hi!"

"Hi!"

There was neither a handshake nor the formal greeting of a kiss. They looked at one another indecisively.

Just a few dozen meters away was the entrance to the public garden, with its cover of leafy trees. They entered, not speaking, walking side by side down a shady pathway, until they came to the bank of a small pond lit by a ray of sun.

They sat on a bench, breathing in the aroma of flowers from the nearby beds and watching in awe as two white swans silently moved across the water.

"So, comrade, what's your name?" These were Célia's first words.

"Luís," he answered.

"Look," she said, smiling. "I came to meet you without even knowing your name, nor anything about you. I'm crazy, don't you think?"

"No, why crazy?"

He thought it was all very natural. They'd met at the demonstration, marched together in the cordon hand in hand, they'd agreed to meet, and now they were there getting to know each other better.

And since she laughed, he added, "Above all, I like you. I liked you right away."

Célia laughed again. "Don't rush things, okay?"

The conversation unfolded easily as they got know one another.

Luís worked at the shipyard. He got there early in the morning, and left at five o'clock. He was a member of the Communist youth group and his political work was also at the shipyard.

Célia also was with the Communist youth, a student in the 12th form with good grades, and she liked studying French, Portuguese literature, and geography.

"So, you see," Luís said after this short introduction, "we have a lot to talk about."

In fact, though, concerning what each of them did, the conversation stopped there. They turned their faces back to the pond, admiring the swans gliding over the bright silver sun-lit water.

They stayed there until it started getting dark.

They made a date for another meeting in the same place, and separated with a gentle but prolonged handshake.

"Be sure you come—"

"Be sure *you* come."

Over the following weeks they continued meeting on Sundays. Without having discussed it, they found themselves alongside the pond but seeking out more isolated spots farther away from the other park visitors.

On the benches they chose, they stopped sitting side by side, and now sat opposite one another looking at each other face to face.

That's how—naturally, inevitably, silently, comfortably but with feeling and for an extended time—they had their first kiss.

They came back every Sunday for their excursions to the garden, gradually finding places that were more and more out of the way. The first kisses almost furtively gave way to trembling embraces, exploration of their bodies, and fusion of their senses.

"This isn't right," Célia said, "at least not here. It can't go on. I don't feel free. Our relationship here is beginning to annoy me."

* * *

They both arrived at the same time, same place. It was a sunny morning.

In a rapid move and with a bright expression, Célia grabbed Luís by the arm. "Come with me!"

"Where?"

"Not to the garden. You'll see. It's not far." She quickened the pace.

Street after street, to Luís it seemed far. Where would she be taking him? The walk seemed interminable. He thought they'd never get there.

"Well?"

"We're close. Very close," Célia repeated.

Finally, on a narrow street, they got to a building like the others, street level and four floors, key in the lock, open the door. They entered. Luís understood.

"Here we are!" Célia said almost in a whisper.

And pressing his arm, she tugged him down the corridor to a living room and a couch.

Célia pulled him closer. They sat together and embraced and kissed, in a crescendo of unrestrained movements searching one another hungrily, he kissing her on the neck, each of them roaming awkwardly, finding more and more nakedness, seconds that seemed like hours, until they drowned in sighs and moans filling the silence of the room and finally a simultaneous deep exhale followed by motionlessness and then silence.

They lay there a long time. Later they put some clothes on and embraced, almost surprised by what had happened. They sat speechless, giving one another fleeting, loving kisses of mutual acknowledgment.

Célia explained where they were—in the house of her older sister Marta, with whom she lived. Marta was separated from her husband, and had a job.

"She's a good girl. She's out today. We can come here whenever she's not here."

That was the beginning of a new, more intimate and deeper relationship. Now their encounters began taking place there in the house. And from the sofa in the living room they moved to Célia's bedroom, Célia's bed, and a nakedness and love without barriers.

One day, by surprise, Marta returned home early, and saw them in bed in Célia's room.

"The mice will play when the cat's away! Who knew?" she exclaimed. "Stay calm, I won't bother you." And she let them be.

"I was stupid," said Célia, getting up. "Don't worry, I'll talk with her."

Luís got dressed, combed his hair and gave her one more kiss. "I got you in trouble."

"It's my fault," she said.

They passed through the living room. Marta was sitting there reading a magazine. She pretended not to see them go by.

Célia led Luís to the door.

"Where should we meet next time?"

"At the garden entrance, like before," Célia proposed, "and I'll be able to tell you how things are here at the house."

Marta showed some displeasure with what had happened. "So, my little hypocrite, already so modern here in this house—you never told me anything. What you did is not nice."

Célia begged her pardon. She recognized she had done something foolish, and was afraid her sister would be angry. But no.

"Do you really love him?" Marta asked.
Yes, she loved him very much.
"And he really loves you?"
Oh, yes, she knew he did.
Well, it could be worked out then. They could meet there in the house. And if he was a serious fellow and had a job, maybe he could come live with them.

That's what happened. Luís, who was already struggling to explain his nights away from his house, told his uncle he was going to be living elsewhere for a while. And he went to live with Célia at Marta's house.

* * *

That arrangement did not last long. Not that the two young people had lost interest in their relationship. And not on account of any issues that might have arisen with Marta.

It was because Luís's political activity had given him a new assignment that would take him out of the country for some time.

Luís distinguished himself at the shipyard for the high quality of his work with the youth. His comrades in the Party observed the young cadre's merit, and chose him, along with two other young men, Manuel and Aníbal, to go to a distant country and take a course of study. As a militant, this task seemed to him like a dream come true.

It would be hard to separate from Célia for almost a year. Still, he thought the time would pass quickly and he'd return to live forever with her. Certainly, he believed, she would understand.

But she did not understand. At the house when, with all due prudence, he told her about the project, Célia didn't want to believe it. "It can't be, you're kidding me."

"No, Célia. It's important, and the Party has already decided."

"The Party, the Party! And me?"

Over the next few days, their exchanges grew tense and dramatic.

"I love you, Célia. You're the most precious thing I have in the world. I beg you to understand."

"No, I do not understand. I gave you everything, and you're abandoning me. I do not forgive you."

What was decided, however, remained decided. In the last weeks, relations between the two deteriorated rapidly. Célia continued to sleep in the same bed with Luís, but rebuffed him with any number of pretexts: to let her sleep on account of a headache, or how tired she was, or because it was her period, and other excuses to avoid him.

"If you're in such a rush to get away, you can leave whenever you want. You need time to get ready for your trip."

But Luís stayed, and only left Marta's house to go to the airport. He said goodbye, kissing Célia tenderly. Coldly, she very nearly refused even a light kiss on her cheek by way of farewell. Seeing his suitcase in hand, as he prepared to leave the bedroom, Célia suddenly changed her attitude and let out a belated cry: "Stay!"

Unable to bear his lover's pain, Luís practically fled from the room. Célia didn't go to the door with him. She stayed standing in her room, paralyzed and frustrated.

With a sense of infinite sadness, Luís felt disgust with himself. He opened the door, then closed it behind him and left.

* * *

The course exposed him to exciting revelations, most of all from the studies themselves. It wasn't only the fact of acquiring knowledge that he never even suspected existed. It was the fresh vision this knowledge gave him, illuminating and interpreting society, nature, the activities he had been involved in up to now, the deepest reasons for being what he already was, a young Communist.

The theory, in the way he studied it, gave him the tools to explain the world and show the ways and the goals for transforming it.

The philosophy equipped him to comprehend the dynamics of material life without resorting to imaginary, invisible higher beings.

His study of economics clarified the fundaments, the origins, the processes and development of the society he was born into, in which he lived, in which he had begun to fight.

And he embraced the ideal of a new society, better, free of exploitation of some human beings by other human beings, where poverty, injustice and oppression were eradicated.

Luís, Manuel and Aníbal exchanged impressions of their studies—what they were learning, the comradeship of their teachers, the hundreds of students with their many languages who attended and lived at the school. And at all the events they went to, the visits to factories, to collective farms, to stores and restaurants, everywhere, they saw the evidence and traces of the society they had imagined, for which, as young Communists, they struggled in their own country.

Luís experienced intensely all these aspects of a different and better world. Wherever they met, he was together with young men and women of other nationalities, as well as of the country where they were staying.

Among them was Conchita, a Mexican girl. On their excursions, and when they were traveling to performances and exhibitions, she was always by his side. One day, when they returned to the school, she unexpectedly made him a casual proposition.

"*Esta noche*, Luís"—she spoke to him in Spanish, knowing he would understand—"tonight I'll be alone in my room. Wouldn't you like to spend it with me?"

Later remembering that moment, Luís had to admit to himself that he looked at her as he never had before and saw the stunning beauty of his comrade, and that at first it occurred to him to accept her tempting invitation. He surprised himself with the words that involuntarily came from his mouth: "No, Conchita, the other comrades are waiting for me."

No one was waiting for him. But in that instant, the memory came to him of Célia's commanding, imploring cry when he left her room: "Stay!"

* * *

Since Luís departed, the atmosphere at Marta's house changed profoundly. Before, Célia was always upbeat and joyful, but now she didn't conceal her gloom. Marta tried to encourage her. "Hey, girl, he's not worth it."

"I don't want to hear about him," Célia replied. "He duped me, so now let him do what he wants."

Marta spoke about her own situation. She married, then her husband left her, and she too wanted nothing more to do with him. "But I didn't let it destroy me, sis, nor sacrifice my happiness. I just started living my own life, that's all."

She made her point even more provocatively. "In the end you'd do well not to love him any more. By now he's going out with other girls."

One day Célia got angry about all the preaching, advice and needling. "What do you think? That I'm still obsessed about him? You judge me wrong. Of course I suffered for being deceived. But more than once I've told you that I don't want anything more from Luís. I've completely discarded any feeling for him."

"That's great," Marta pretended to believe her. "In that case everything will be much easier."

Such talk just about evaporated when the two sisters took off for the Algarve for their summer vacation. Marta got hold of a tent and sleeping bags and a huge blue umbrella, and they went.

The beach, the sun and the ocean water made them forget everything else. They smeared themselves with sun lotion, spread out their colorful towels on the sand and, with sunglasses over their eyes, stretched out in the sun to tan.

Before midday they rose and ran into the ocean. Marta dove and swam with gusto. Célia entered the water timidly, keeping her feet on the ocean floor and hopping over the waves as they rolled in.

The two women got out of the water, ran and wiped themselves off with the colorful towels, and once again, dark glasses shading their eyes, lay out to dry in the sun.

They ate something in a cheap restaurant, dozed off back in their tent, and in the late afternoon returned to the beach, sheltering under their sunshade.

That's how the first days of their vacation went. Then their beach life took on a new dimension.

While Marta was swimming, a young man dove into the water and emerged next to Célia, who was playing with the waves. He had a cute face. He asked a question and made an offer: "You don't know how to swim? I can teach you, do you want me to?"

Célia shook her head no.

The boy went back to his diving, and Célia watched for him to reappear. She waited and waited until, rather anxiously, she thought something might have happened to him. But he rose out of the water some distance away and with an uplifted arm waved goodbye.

Célia told her sister what had happened.

"You're a jerk," Marta told her. "You can see he swims well, and he could teach you. Finally you'd learn to swim."

The next morning, the same scene recurred. The boy appeared next to Célia out of the water. He laughed and his handsome face lit up. "Shall we?" he asked, pointing to the water.

Célia asked what she needed to do. He explained, and demonstrated how to swim lying flat in the water. "Come with me now. Don't be afraid. I'll hold you by the chin and support you."

They stepped farther into the water. The boy was a good teacher. And returning her to her feet, he took off. "See you tomorrow!"

"See?" Marta commented when they laid themselves out in the sun. "You're finally getting the knack of it."

Célia agreed. She started learning fast. Only one thing bothered her. The young fellow supported her by her chin and kept her at the surface holding her by the waist.

Marta broke out laughing. "What would you prefer? To hold you by your feet?"

For the next three days the boy came regularly, continuing to give her lessons, and she learned quickly. But on the fourth day, the teacher went too far, not just supporting her but feeling her indecently.

Célia ran out of the water at once and told her sister about it.

"Oh, you little innocent creature you," she said. "Look how good-looking that guy is. If it was me, I'd feel lucky."

Célia was angry, and the final days of vacation she didn't go back into the ocean.

The boldly likable boy went to look for her as she tanned herself next to the blue umbrella. "What happened? Are you sick?"

"Leave me alone," she answered in a rotten mood.

"But—"

"Go away. And don't come by again." With that she turned her back to the sun.

*   *   *

The youths who had gone to take the course returned, full of impressions, memories and presents.

A comrade from the Party and another from the Communist Youth leadership welcomed them at the airport and brought them directly to the Party Center. There they all had a talk. The young men related what they had studied and learned, and the excursions they took.

They, in turn, were updated on what the Party was planning for them. Luís would continue working at the military shipyard and would become part of the youth leadership. Manuel and Aníbal would head out by train that same night for Coimbra and Porto, where they would resume their previous activities.

When the meeting ended, Luís ran to drop his suitcase off at his aunt and uncle's house where he had lived before moving in at Marta's.

After the welcome-home embraces and words, he wanted to go out, but they wouldn't let him. They had a whole feast ready for him, and wanted him to tell them all about the course, the impressions he brought back of the country, the people and the comrades, and made him stay for dinner.

Finally, his uncle rose from the table. "You must be tired. Go to bed and sleep well. We'll have time later to talk more."

No, he couldn't, Luís contradicted him. He still had to go out.

"At this hour?" his uncle said with surprise. "Leave it for tomorrow."

"I won't be long." Luís quickly removed a package from his suitcase, asked for the key to the street door so as not to wake them when he returned and, quite intending not to come back, left in a hurry.

Marta's house wasn't far away. With a certain nervousness, he knocked on the door, once, twice, three times, anxiously anticipating seeing Célia again and spending the night. No one answered. For sure, no one was home. Where would they have gone? Surprised, unhappy, disappointed, he went back to the street. He walked a few steps, then turned around and knocked on the door again. Maybe they hadn't answered because they were asleep. Twice he rang the doorbell, the last time strong and loud. The silence convinced him no one was home.

A thousand hypothetical explanations occurred to him, all of them dark.

In a state of both excitement and exhaustion, he returned to his aunt and uncle's house, lay down, slept uneasily, awoke early, got dressed and left, all before his relatives got up.

He was going to present himself early at work in the shipyard, where he knew they were awaiting him.

But, senselessly, he detoured from his route once again to knock on Marta's door. No one.

* * *

That morning Luís resumed his work at the shipyard. He finished his workday, then gathered with the young comrades for a pleasant, unrushed reunion.

Leaving the shipyard, he ran to Célia's school. Maybe the school year had started already. But that was another disappointment—the school was still locked up.

For several weeks he suffered the same disappointments. He went to work on time and was a good worker, met with his comrades, and assigned tasks. Not once did he fall short of his duties.

Once or twice a week he went to knock on Marta's door with the vague hope that they had returned home. He tried reassuring himself with other thoughts—could they have gone back to their hometown to spend time with their parents? Was she still on holiday at the beach?

Tired by now, and resigned to a chance meeting at best, he knocked on the door once more. This time it opened, and he saw Célia standing before him, beautiful as always, but restrained, hesitating to let him in.

"Célia!" He moved to embrace her.

She backed away. "Come in, then," she said coldly.

They had barely entered the living room when Marta appeared, speaking loudly. "You here? Who would have guessed! Sit down, have a seat. I'll leave you two alone." And she left as she had entered.

Célia sat across from him at a certain distance, and her words came out with dry iciness, as if to say as little as possible. "Have you been well?"

"Célia! I don't understand you. I'm sorry, I just don't understand."

"It's easy to understand," she answered with even greater frigidity. "Everything's over between us."

Luís felt like he'd been punched. He placed on the floor the package he had carried with him as a souvenir every time he tried to find her. "Can I know the reason?" he asked quietly.

"The reason doesn't concern you. What I had to say I have said."

"I don't want to know anything you don't want to tell me. But let's not leave it like this. You're saying I should leave and we won't be seeing each other again. Is that what you want?"

Célia's tone of voice softened. She had thought quite a lot. Not acquiescing to her request that he stay, he left her for a trip abroad, where possibly he had what for him were mere escapades.

"Célia!—" he interrupted.

"Let me speak, Luís." She continued. No, she was not interested in resuming any kind of connection with him. Neither did she need to give any further explanations.

"We could meet, Célia. As comrades, as friends. We can give it time."

"No, Luís. I continue to be your comrade. What you did to me could have shaken my convictions. But no. I remain a Communist. But I don't care to see you again. None of our assignments will bring us together as comrades. Meeting with you as comrades makes no sense. That's all, Luís."

Having said which, she got up from her chair to end the visit.

"I brought a...a souvenir for you," Luís stammered, picking up the package.

"Keep it, keep it. Keep it for somebody else." She opened the door and let him out.

Luís left, overtaken by infinite desolation.

And Célia, as soon as he left, threw herself on the sofa and wept.

"Now this?" her sister reacted. "Don't be an idiot, Célia."

* * *

Would it have been possible, as Luís proposed at the end of the conversation, for the two of them to continue meeting but only as comrades? Naturally not work-related meetings, but personal? Or was Célia right to reject them, saying they didn't make sense?

The two sisters exchanged opinions on these questions.

Marta's view was categorical. After they had separated, meetings between the two of them as friends would be not only ambiguous but unviable. That's what happened with her.

"And as you know, that's what happens with me," said Célia.

Marta was not done with the conversation, however. "Yes, that's true, Célia. I told you many times that I never thought about my husband again. Not long ago I completely agreed with you when you said encounters with Luís as comrades wouldn't work."

She hesitated briefly, and added, "But at the end of the day, I lied to you and I lied to myself. The truth is that I hurt a lot, and the separation was very hard on me."

Like Marta, Célia also hesitated a little. Then she decided to tell the truth. "I'm hurting too. A lot."

"Later," Marta said further, "I felt free and I learned to take care of myself. That's what you have to do, sis."

Célia closed the conversation defensively. "That's not my business, understand? I just don't want to talk about it any more."

* * *

There's another demonstration on the Avenue. The youth are participating in full strength. Red flags, colorful banners, songs, slogans, joy, struggle, confidence.

In front of the sound car, from side to side across the wide street, a cordon forms of young men and women. Luís sees Célia amongst a clutch of girls. He runs to grasp her hand. "Come!"

He pulls her. She hesitates. Then she decides. The two run to join the cordon.

From time to time, hand in hand, they look at one another, shout the slogans, making a harmony of two in the general chorus.

The march ends. They remain another moment holding hands.

"Shall we get together?" Luís asks.

She hesitates again.

"Célia! Célia!" her girlfriends call.

"Shall we get together?" Luís repeats.

Célia lets go of her comrade's hand, runs to join up with her friends, stops a moment, turns around and, before melting into the mass of young people, cries out to Luís, "Come by!"

Parallel Stories

1

AT morning's end, Pedro mortared a few more bricks in the wall around old Baltazar's modest home and knocked off work.

Just at that moment, the old man opened the door of his house with his shirt open and called out jovially, "So, boy, going to lunch?"

"It's time, Senhor Baltazar," Pedro answered. "I'll fill up and then I'll come back."

"Eat hearty, boy, you need it."

Pedro put down his spade and tray, washed his hands at a faucet in the little yard, grabbed a plastic bag and left.

When he got to the Party Center, he headed to the barroom, where just one other old man was being served. With no one else around, the room was silent, empty and still.

Vanda, of the wide smile and young features, waited on him. "The usual sandwich?"

Smiling too, he nodded yes. "And a glass of red."

Vanda expertly prepared a sandwich of major proportions for him: bread, tomato slices, cheese and ham.

She handed it to Pedro, came out from behind the counter and the two of them sat at the only table in the bar.

Pedro had a healthy appetite. Vanda watched him, amused and wondering if he'd be able to finish the whole sandwich.

He was able to, naturally. When he'd done eating, he pulled a small transistor radio out of his bag. First there was music, then the news.

"Did you hear?" Pedro suddenly exclaimed. "Did you hear that?"

"What was it?" Vanda asked, not having noticed anything that would stir up such amazement.

"The government has decided to import thousands of tons of potatoes!"

"And?"

"And so the farmers in our district won't be able to sell theirs."

Resolved to take action, Pedro wanted to know the opinion of Gonçalo, a member of the District Committee and a comrade of greater experience. He asked Vanda if he had been to the Center that morning, or if she knew when he might be coming by.

"Only in the evening," she replied.

Leaving the Center, Pedro went back to work on the wall at old Baltazar's house, and as it started getting dark, he returned to the Party Center to talk with Gonçalo. Vanda joined the conversation.

They agreed it was necessary to do something—warn the farmers, and try to organize their struggle. But how, if they didn't have contact with them?

Vanda remembered something: The following Sunday was the District Fair. They could print up a leaflet and go to the fair and distribute it. "Maybe produce it at the *Sorzelo News* printshop," she suggested.

"Don't even think about it, my friend," said Gonçalo. "Comrade Fradique has already stated that he'd never use his little printshop for Party manifestos. His son—who's the typesetter and not a Communist—also would not agree to print them."

"Then maybe at the workshop of Manuel dos Pregos," Pedro offered. "He prints business cards and advertising flyers for the stores around here." That was a good idea.

"Should we invite Joana to go with us?" Vanda proposed, glancing over to the counter at the bar where she was tidying up the glasses and plates.

Yes, agreed. And maybe her husband Hermínio could go with them too.

The decision made, they went into action. Gonçalo drew up a statement, and Pedro went to Manuel dos Pregos to arrange for the print job. At the Center they painted a huge poster. They were ready to take action alongside the farmers at the fair.

2

That summer morning, fairgoers streamed from the road into the vast fairgrounds—carts, pickup trucks, thin horses led by ropes, a few heifers, bicycles with huge packs on their luggage racks, and people on foot not carrying anything.

At the entrance to the fair, high up on the faded wall of a ruined cookie factory, an excited group was putting up a sign with big letters: "Against the import of potatoes!"

Mounting a fragile wooden ladder that Gonçalo was holding, Pedro had a can of glue and a brush in his hands. He was having trouble unfolding and gluing the poster.

"Careful, Pedro!" Vanda shouted, seeing the young man losing his balance for a moment.

"It's done!" he called jubilantly from on high, and started descending the ladder.

With the sign up, the group placed the ladder against the factory wall and started handing out their little flyers.

Quiet Hermínio, standing in place, handed them out to people who passed by. Joana, next to him, did the same. Pedro scurried here and there, approaching the fairgoers and always saying a few words. Raising his voice above the ever-present noise of fairgoers pushing through with their vehicles and cattle, Gonçalo also walked around tirelessly, singling out this one and that one, briefly explaining what the flyer said. Vanda distributed her flyers in a whirlwind of arms extended to the carts and with a permanent, natural smile and a couple of words. Her youth and good humor made the task easy.

Pedro was the first to finish. "Gonçalo," he said to his comrade, "I'm just going to go over and see if there are any more manifestos left." And he ran off.

The few he brought back were quickly handed out. Gonçalo hoisted the ladder to his shoulder and the five comrades walked back to the Party Center.

3

By contrast with the hubbub and noise at the fair, a peaceful quiet reigned in the square in front of City Hall.

On the esplanade across from the square, people sipped on their coffees and beers.

At one of those tables three members of the Party's District Committee, Pratas, Fradique and Santos, sat conversing in guarded voices. They had already received the news—and some anonymous person had brought them a copy of the manifesto.

"What do the comrades want?" Fradique opened. "A fair is just a fair, not a political demonstration. That poster and the distribution of this manifesto—both foolish! Don't you think so, Dr. Pratas?"

"You're right, it is foolish. That kind of agitation only creates problems for us."

The next day on the esplanade, the three returned to the subject. They couldn't leave it alone. "If we don't take a public position," said Pratas, "we leave ourselves in apparent support of that stupid action, and our *dear comrades* will call it a victory and go on doing their own thing."

It was time to end any misunderstanding. A critique of the distribution of that flyer at the fair needed to be issued.

Fradique had a proposal apropos. He could write and publish an article about the events. And he could do so with complete freedom. By virtue of an inheritance from an uncle, he was—and had been since he was a young man—the owner, director and effectively the sole editor of the *Sorzelo News*. That's when he changed his name. Francisco Coninhas was not a suitable name for the masthead of the paper, and as the author's signature on stories and editorials. He had chosen the name Fradique and, over the many years since the paper had been coming out, all recall of his true name had been lost.

Now, in light of what had happened at the fair, he'd already formulated some fundamental ideas he would defend in the newspaper.

First, that a fair is a fair and not a place for political demonstrations.

"Exactly!" Pratas agreed. "For the Party to appear at the fair and engage in agitation creates strong resistance and even hostility in relation to the Party."

The second idea, Fradique proceeded, was that such agitation disturbed the conditions of social peace indispensable for solving the problems in the district.

"Right!" Pratas said in support. And he added, "Furthermore, such action in the name of the Party raises legitimate objections from the mayor and compromises our good relations with him."

Santos listened to his comrades, but said nothing.

"How about you, Santos, you're not saying anything?" Pratas asked.

"I'm in agreement, clearly," Santos answered without further elaboration.

A week later, the article was published in a special edition of the *Sorzelo News*.

The newspaper counted on a steady stable of subscribers, who read it because it was the only one that published local news and announcements.

The internal situation in the Party, that Fradique's article revealed, spread quickly across town, evoking a wide variety of comments.

"There's just a few of them left." "With one against another, they'll be even fewer." "It won't be long before they disappear." Such was the general tenor of what people said.

4

One day when Pedro returned to work after lunch, old Baltazar appeared at the door and told him to come into the house. "Come here, young man. I want to have a talk." And he led him in.

"This is how I live," he began, showing him the house—a clean, well-organized kitchen, a little living room, two bedrooms, and a bathroom with an overhead shower.

He sat him down and explained why he had called him in. Since his parents had died, and then his wife and his son, he lived by himself. He alone took care of the house and didn't need any help with the domestic chores. But it wasn't easy living alone. Evenings were long and lonely. The silence in the house, and his solitude, had gotten hard to bear.

"What can you do, my boy? The years are weighing heavily on me."

He'd seen Pedro working, so carefully and seriously at what he did, and he reminded him of his son. So the idea came to him to offer him a place to live in the house. Nothing would change in his life. Pedro needn't be wary. Old Baltazar would continue to pay him his wages for building the wall around the house.

Old Baltazar said all this in a calm and friendly manner, without showing any emotion, as though he were speaking with a friend of long years' duration.

The conversation went further, and Pedro ended up accepting the offer.

"All right, so I'll come and live with you. I'll continue working on the wall, and you'll continue to pay me. But for my part, I'll pay you the same rent that I'm paying now for my room. Okay?"

That's exactly what Old Baltazar was hoping for. "Okay!"

5

Pratas took the floor at the District Committee meeting. What happened on the day of the fair, according to him, had to be analyzed. Who could be so sure that importing potatoes would jeopardize the farmers of the district selling theirs? Furthermore, contrary to what some of the comrades were saying, the action of the poster and leaflets led to the farmers pulling away from the Party and it created an unhealthy instability which didn't help solve the problems of the district. Besides which, who on the District Committee authorized that action?

Gonçalo countered. It's our comrades here who should explain who approved publication of the article in the *Sorzelo News* condemning the action that took place at the fair, and discrediting the Party in front of the farmers. Who authorized them to raise in the media, concretely in the *Sorzelo News*, issues concerning the internal life of the Party? The correct course was to continue the struggle against the importation of potatoes. The distribution of the flyer had been an important contribution toward alerting the farmers.

Pratas did not give in, nor was he persuaded. "There's more, my friend," he replied. "You should know that your initiative provoked serious criticism from the mayor. He was furious when he heard about it."

"So there, you see what happened?" Fradique stressed.

"Yes, that's the issue, and it's good you said it," Pedro jumped in. "The issue is that we should not surrender our direct ties to the people, and to the people's struggle, to an understanding with the mayor, Silva Penedo."

"So, Comrade Pedro has spoken!" Pratas roared with laughter.

"Yes, the absolute truth!" Fradique laughed too.

And they shrugged their shoulders, as if to say, *Talk all you want, but you're full of crap.*

Pratas laughed, but he was clearly irritated by Pedro's observation. The comrades, he added, were not taking reality into account. The potato producers were from rural parishes far from town, very reactionary small farmers controlled by the priests and to whom Communists were literal devils. They came into town with their carts to buy and sell, and nothing else concerned them. The comrades should remember there weren't even bus routes that linked the district seat to those parishes. The mayor long ago had a plan to address that situation, but the problems were so great that he abandoned it.

"What you're saying is crystal clear," said Gonçalo. "In the end you want us to refrain from defending the vital interests of the farmers in the district. Because your main concern is your relations with the mayor."

The argument went on like that and reached no consensus.

"We can't make up our mind," said Hermínio. "Let's go have something to eat. It's time."

6

They all ate in the barroom, where there was little available—just the usual sandwiches and drinks.

Joana and Vanda waited professionally on Pratas, Fradique and Santos, who ordered what they wanted in the same cool, distant tone they would use with the waiters at a café. With Gonçalo, Pedro and Hermínio, with any one of them, it was different, and with Hermínio not just because he was Joana's husband. With these they spoke with visible friendliness in the pleasure of their company.

So it was that day, by habit. One group continued conversing with them even as they ate, and the others restricted themselves to asking for what they wanted and went on talking amongst themselves.

The difference in the way they conducted themselves did not go unnoticed. So much so that one day Pratas said to his two friends, "This is too much—two women at the Center and they're both from the Orthodox party faction. For now we have to put up with it since we don't have any other women. But as soon as possible, we have to deal with it."

7

The very next day, Pratas was once again the first to speak. He had a prepared lecture, launching the discussion on new matters. He said that the working class was disappearing, that the old proletariat was vanishing, that the social composition of society had changed, that the idea of the working class as the vanguard was completely eclipsed by history, and that because of all these societal transformations, intellectuals were now called upon to play that role.

Gonçalo answered. The issues Pratas raised were not new. They've been under discussion for years now. Those, like Pratas, who offered them up now as innovative thinking were objectively negating the class character of the Party and denying the very reason for its existence.

There certainly have been profound social changes. But an exploited, wage-earning class still existed, apart from the vast numbers of people in the country's working class by anyone's definition.

Pulling his thin, myopic face into a frown, Fradique spoke up to reinforce Pratas's opinion. "Are you in the working class, Gonçalo? You, who were laid off with hundreds of other workers from the bankrupt cookie factory, and now you're working as a handyman or temp worker in a bicycle workshop? And you, Hermínio, are you a trained worker or a technical engineer? Out of all of you, Pedro is the only worker, because he's in civil construction. But even he doesn't have steady work. So one out of six members is enough to declare that the Party is the party of the working class?"

"Before anything else, comrade," Gonçalo hit back, "will you tell me what class I belong to? Did I cease to be a worker for being laid off? For changing my job? And furthermore, it's in the united action of factory and other workers, farmers, the general population, in the defense of their own interests and rights, that the nature of our Party's class is shown, as a party of the working class and of all workers."

"Clear as day," Pedro concluded. "In effect, what the comrades want is to put the Party at the beck and call of the mayor, and maybe also earn the good graces of the Viana family, the richest people in the district, with whom Mayor Silva Penedo is lips and teeth."

This was too much. Pratas lost his temper. "Me with the Vianas? That is an insult, my friend, and I do not tolerate insults. I demand that you retract what you said!"

"On this issue," Pedro replied, "you are capable of making a dozen speeches and writing a dozen articles. I understand you're shocked by what I said. But your true thinking—your concrete positions in concrete cases—shows that you are not with the workers and wage-earners in general, but with the bourgeoisie."

The argument devolved into vengeful words from which there was no exit, and the meeting broke apart in open conflict.

Still, before he departed, Pratas turned around and yelled, "You must take back what you said, Pedro. I demand it!"

8

It's understandable why Pratas could not admit the reference to the Vianas.

The Vianas were indeed the *grands seigneurs* of Sorzelo. They owned the only "palace" in town. They had a number of house servants, and a beautiful large garden next to their mansion. They had an expensive car and belonged to a club only for the biggest snobs. Their silent, reclusive lifestyle was likely meant to downplay their immense fortune but only served to reveal it.

No one saw their faces in public—not in any café, nor public event, not even at the pharmacy. They created a totally secretive life for themselves, admitting to their company, to their house and their club, only the most carefully selected moneyed people.

Their children studied at the University, spent their school time in the city and their vacation time at the beach with friends. Only at Christmastime did they appear in Sorzelo, shocking and frightening the population with the deafening rumble and dizzying speed of their motorcycles such as no one had ever seen before.

The source of such a sizable fortune in this relatively small region gave rise to much argument. Some said their wealth dated back a long time and spoke of many generations of nobility. One day someone mentioned that the oldest of the Viana clan was a baron.

But the older people in town disavowed such fantasies. Long ago, according to them, a certain Roberto Viana emigrated to Brazil in search of the money tree and, unlike so many others who returned poor and sick just to die in their own land, this one came back filthy rich. But how he acquired his fortune no one knew.

That the mayor was welcomed into the Viana house and club was well-known. But the same could not be said of Pratas. It was whispered—although he had never bragged of it—that he had refused an invitation to visit the club.

In the heat of the discussion, when he referred to the relations between Pratas and the Vianas in the terms he used, Pedro had certainly gone too far.

9

The hour came to close up the Center. As the meeting ended, Pratas once again insisted that Pedro retract what he said and ask forgiveness. Pedro pretended not to hear the demand.

Under this foreboding cloud, everyone said goodnight and left.

Santos and Gonçalo left together. They lived on the same street and continued talking along the way. It was a unique situation. They did not speak of conflicting views nor their differences of opinion as to Party activity. They managed to get along conversing about very general subjects—the weather, events of the day, their personal tastes in plants, animals and natural environments.

Fradique left with Pratas in the latter's car, continuing their talk about what they had been debating.

Hermínio and his wife Joana left without talking. Pedro was the last. He left with Vanda and, as was their custom, walked her home.

It was a pleasant, peaceful summer night, and they conversed as they ambled along. Not about the Party, or the arguments and misunderstandings. But about themselves, two human beings, Pedro and Vanda.

As they proceeded, they passed Misericórdia Square, casually glanced at the lighted windows at the Vianas' club, and stopped for a moment.

Vanda turned to her friend. "You seem sad, Pedro. What's happening with you?"

"Nothing special, Vanda."

Aside from the conflict in the Party, he himself didn't know. It wasn't sadness so much as dissatisfaction.

"Are you tired of me? Is that it?"

How could she think that? If he felt anything was missing, it was not getting together with her even more, and not only at the Party Center or when he walked her home. He'd like it if they could meet out in the sun and fresh air with no set time they had to return.

The course of the conversation led to Pedro's proposal, which she accepted: One Sunday when they were free, to go out to the countryside. Not far from Sorzelo were some lovely spots and beautiful landscapes.

As they considered their plan, the night advanced without their noticing the time. The streets, almost deserted at that hour, wrapped the two youngsters in their mutual enchantment.

They got to the door of Dona Leonilde's house, the town seamstress where both Vanda and Isabel lived and worked.

Dona Leonilde agreed that Vanda could continue living with her even as she was spending the better part of her time at the Party. Vanda couldn't invite Pedro to enter.

"You know? Dona Leonilde is not a bad lady. And my sister is truly a lovely girl, but don't hold it against them that they don't understand us."

"It's okay," Pedro said. "*We* should understand *them*."

"You're such a kind person, Pedro."

And for the first time, she kissed him on his cheek. She opened the door, turned around again and said goodbye with her open hand in a gentle, loving gesture. Pedro also gestured goodbye.

"Good night. Sleep well."

10

It always happened that it was above all Gonçalo and Pratas who, confronting one another, expounded the main arguments at the meetings. There were reasons for that.

During the time of the dictatorship, Gonçalo was a worker at the cookie factory which, after it went belly-up, closed its doors and threw almost the entire workforce out of work. He stood out in the democratic unity movement and was the only citizen of Sorzelo to be arrested by the PIDE and taken to Lisbon. Only for a week, but long enough in the town to be deemed the most distinguished opponent of the régime.

Pratas too participated in the Opposition. A teacher—who did not hold classes—he lived comfortably off his rental income. He never hid his ideas. He was never arrested but he was well-known, especially considering his social position as the most outstanding democrat in Sorzelo, which he considered himself to be.

It's not clear what it was, after the April 25th Revolution, that led these two men to emerge in the light of day as Communists and to take the initiative of opening a Party headquarters in a house belonging to Gonçalo's brother, who had emigrated abroad.

Soon a number of comrades they had not known about joined them. Pedro, enthusiastic and with youthful energy, along with Vanda, his neighbor, with her eyes open to life. Then there was the couple Hermínio and Joana. Then came Santos, a technical engineer, which surprised everyone when he showed up. And then yet another surprise—Fradique, from the *Sorzelo News*, after a few exploratory visits to the Party Center. Those people comprised the District Committee, there being no other militants.

Everyone participated in the discussions. Pedro showed a sharp and audacious critical mind, Fradique a highly developed and sarcastic reflective thoughtfulness. Hermínio rarely spoke up but always made good sense. Santos limited himself to agreeing. But the main lines of argument normally fell to Gonçalo and Pratas, and this was recognized by all as the natural order.

11

When everyone left the Center, Gonçalo returned home one night discontented after their meeting. He left with Santos, and they had walked together in silence before separating.

His wife Alice was waiting for him, patient and endearing as always, without affecting her very independent stance as her own woman.

She never uttered a word of censure toward her husband, not even when, although rarely, he came home quite late at night. She wasn't in the Party. She hadn't even once gone to the Party Center and showed no inclination to do so.

"You're a Communist," she said one day to her husband, "and I have nothing against it. On the contrary. But I have no more interest in your activities today than I ever did. You can do your propaganda in the Party, fine, because you're a Communist. But here in this house, I am the Party!"

And, feeling good about herself, she added with a smile, "You can't say I don't treat you well. If anything, I smother you with affection."

Such was the ambiance at Gonçalo's house, the home of a deeply committed couple still very much in love.

"Tired?" she asked that night when he came in, and she kissed him.

"Tired? Yes, it was a very difficult meeting."

"They're going to kill you, those friends of yours." And she asked if he wanted anything to eat.

He said no, but she added, "Well, I'll give you a hot tea before you go to bed, okay?"

Gonçalo smiled. "You know, I just said I didn't want to eat anything, but what do you have?"

Alice brought out some codfish cakes that were left over from the midday meal. "Next time please let me know. I'll make you dinner."

"It's fine, Alice. Those cakes are really delicious."

"Sorry there aren't more of them."

Having said which, Alice opened a drawer and pulled out an envelope. "I have some news for you, Gonçalo. A letter came from your brother in Germany."

She opened the envelope, unfolded the letter and read. "He's just asking for news from us. As far as the house is concerned, you can continue using it for Party headquarters. He's a true friend, your brother," she observed.

12

One day, a beautiful blue car with a high cylinder capacity stopped in front of City Hall.

On the other side of the square, at the café on the esplanade, many people rose excitedly from their tables to see better. Some applauded.

"Bravo!" commented Fradique. "It's about time there's some dignity to the office of the mayor."

That way of looking at it did not appease everyone. Even there on the esplanade, City Hall's purchase of the blue car came up for heated discussion.

"It's not a question of being a good car. That's all right," said one onlooker. "But to choose a model that's so extravagant is what's foolish. Look, the Vianas' car is no less fine a car—and they're the richest people around—and is probably even more deluxe and expensive, but it doesn't call so much attention to itself. It's a dark color, and an ordinary design."

Talk arose about the blue car also at the Party Center, and Fradique maintained his position. "Authority and the exercise of power require a corresponding public image. It's a matter of dignity."

"No," Gonçalo answered. "The dignity of a mayor is not in the ostentatiousness of his image, but in the decency of his spending, when money is so needed to solve the very serious problems in the district—"

"So what do you want?" Pratas interrupted. "That the mayor go around on a bicycle from the shop where you work?"

"A good car, yes," said Gonçalo, "but not that shocking blue beauty. If you approve of that purchase, does that mean you would do the same if you were mayor?"

The talk grew ever more sour.

"You are a bunch of poverty pimps, and at least in theory our Party is a party that does seek to gain power," Pratas pronounced. "Wealth and wellbeing are necessary for society, and you defend the general immiseration of all."

"The acceptance of wealth for the rich and misery for the people is in actuality *your* idea," Gonçalo said. "And since you are clearly taking this conversation onto an unfortunate path, I'm sorry, but let's go there. Tell us, Comrade Pratas, do you think it's okay to drive around in Silva Penedo's blue car?"

"Me?"

"Yes, you, comrade. I saw you yesterday."

"You didn't see right. You must have seen me in my car."

"Your car is very nice, comrade. But don't think it compares, or could be confused with the blue car. I saw perfectly well. You were in the blue car side by side with Silva Penedo."

"And what of it?" Pratas exploded, having no other response to offer.

"A lot! People see you two driving around side by side in the blue car and will say the Party is collaborating with Silva Penedo making outrageous purchases at City Hall."

Without knowing what more to say, Pratas reverted to his old, clumsy irony. "All right then, Gonçalo, next time I'll ask you to supply a bicycle from your workshop."

"And do you know how to ride it?" Pedro asked, laughing.

13

On Flowers Street, in a poor neighborhood, a large open hole in the pavement had been there for a long time without being fixed. It was a danger to anyone who came along.

More than once the residents had gone to City Hall to demand urgent repairs. The mayor never spoke with them. The response from a functionary had always been the same: "The necessary measures have already been taken."

And the hole remained, just waiting for the first accident. Until one day, what could have been avoided happened.

A boy running at play didn't see the hole, fell in and was badly hurt, suffering a broken leg.

People came running. While some took the boy to the hospital, other residents assembled to protest the negligence.

"Let the mayor come and see! Let the mayor come and see!" they shouted.

Time passed and no one left the scene. "Let the mayor come and see! Let the mayor come and see!" they insisted.

Finally, a City Hall employee arrived. The crowd hushed in expectation. The timid man cleared his throat and with a forced self-importance said, "Senhor Mayor has asked me to tell you the necessary measures have already been taken."

What the hell! He was repeating precisely the same words that they had heard over and over again in previous complaints.

An angry cry of protest and shouting rose up. In one brief moment of quiet, a voice was heard: "People! He's not coming. Let's go to City Hall!"

That call corresponded so exactly to the way people were feeling that everyone followed it with a clamor through the streets.

When the crowd arrived, two soldiers from the National Republican Guard—the GNR—were already posted at the City Hall door.

One demonstrator, the same one from the neighborhood who had made the call to march, approached the functionary who came to the door. "We came from Flowers Street and we want to meet with the mayor."

"I'll see," the flunky answered, terrified by the shouts of protest.

After a long time, with neither mayor nor City Hall flunky showing up, the protests started up again.

The functionary reappeared with a response. The mayor would not come out to speak with them. But he was available to receive a delegation of three or four demonstrators. Those who happened to be in front, closest to the door, rushed in.

14

On the esplanade on the other side of the plaza, the customers barely made the effort to get up and see, and quickly sat down again. They saw the scene and heard the shouting of the crowd. Truthfully, they were shocked and alarmed, but they continued to sip their coffees and beers as though nothing were happening.

"Did you see?" Fradique asked Pratas. "Did you see who was at the front of the crowd and entered with some of the others? No less than our *dear comrade* Pedro."

Pratas tried to maintain his imperturbable face, but his words could not hide his nervousness and unrest. "I just hope, " he said, reining in his emotions, "that Silva Penedo won't be stupid enough to give in to disorder."

"If you get to him in time," Fradique advised, "it might be good to go see him tomorrow morning and see if they've fixed the problem."

"Right. I'll try. Unfortunately we have comrades who only create problems for us. What do they seek to achieve stirring up commotion? They want the revolution? They don't learn from history. They're an echo from the past."

A few days later it was learned that the mayor had ordered work on filling the hole on Flowers Street to begin immediately, and that he would go there himself when the job was completed.

"Coward," Pratas commented.

"We must discuss all this in the Party," Fradique added.

"I can already hear what Gonçalo and company will conclude," Pratas continued. "They'll conclude that it's worth the effort to struggle and that through struggle they will achieve results and victories. I'm sure that's what they'll say."

"It's easy to combat such conclusions," Fradique offered. "What the facts show is that agitation and disorder only create unhealthy conflict with City Hall, jeopardizing the good relations we have with them."
"Exactly," Pratas agreed.

15

Fradique rose, washed himself with cold water, went to the veranda and performed a few gymnastic exercises, breathing deeply of the fresh morning air. Slender and slight, he showed a surprising agility. When he finished, he placed his spectacles with thick lenses and white metal frames on his nose and seated himself at the table to have his breakfast.

Gracinda, his attractive, fine-featured wife, entered impetuously and ill-tempered. Her charming face contrasted shockingly with her acid words. "Great! You don't even set the table. What am I around here? Just someone to take care of you? Aren't I good for anything else?"

With his small face, thin and wrinkled, his twinkling eyes and quick words, Fradique did not appear impressed. "Go on, my dove, don't be upset and bring me my coffee."

"Bring your coffee, bring your coffee. You only know how to give orders. All you do is sit and read and write, run the newspaper and make that poor son of yours compose it for printing in the typography office. How about the slave who works in the house, who serves you your dinner—and after all that, there you go again into your cave to read and write."

"Okay, enough already with your lamentations. And don't criticize your son working in the typography. Or would you rather he go around like a vagabond? I've already told you I spend time with my friends. You know very well I'm a Communist, Gracinda, you have to get used to it. Besides—"

"Besides what? You just like your own comfort and convenience. You're very intelligent, I won't deny. But your intelligence doesn't entitle you to hang about with serious people. You could just as well be accepted into the Vianas' club. But no, you're only comfortable with people who don't amount to anything. This is not going to end well, Fradique. For sure, it won't end well."

"Go on, forget all that and serve me my coffee. It'll be cold soon."

Gracinda served him his coffee, quickly drank her own, rose from the table and left.

"Whew!" Fradique sighed.

It's hard to say who was right. She was a grouch and he was smug and complacent. They were always going at one another. All the accusations they made were justified. But for years they had lived like that, as though, ironically, their incessant arguments were their expression of understanding. She returned to the kitchen and began her household chores. He went into his office to scrupulously prepare the speech he was going to make later that day at the District Committee.

He had to show who he was. For the first time, it would be he, not Pratas, who would open the discussion.

16

At the meeting, Fradique, with his face drawn and his eyes glinting behind his thick lenses, made grave accusations.

We need to discuss the activities of Gonçalo, Pedro and Hermínio. As he saw it, they had acted as a group at the fair and created serious problems in the Party's relations with the mayor. They had provoked a riot on Flowers Street. And at all times the three appeared to be colluding to oppose positions, resolutions and decisions by himself—Fradique—Pratas and Santos. What else was needed to consider it proven that the three were pursuing factional activity in open violation of the by-laws?

"Proven!" Pratas exclaimed.

The esplanade boys had come in for the kill, but the argument went the other way.

Gonçalo took the floor. He expressed agreement that it was time to debate the issue. Because the accusation against himself— Gonçalo—Pedro and Hermínio, of conducting factional activity not only was not proven, but the person making the accusation is the one who was conducting activity that could be considered as such.

As for himself, Pedro and Hermínio, they coincided in the defense of the Party and the expansion of mass work. But they did not have separate meetings as an organized group.

"If there is factional work, it's you that are doing it. You, concretely you, Pratas, you, Fradique, and you, Santos. And furthermore, you didn't even hide it. You met on the esplanade on the square, and that's where you made decisions and agreed how you'd operate within and outside the Party."

"Liar!" Pratas shouted. "Don't invent phantoms. If you're making accusations, you have to offer specific instances."

"I'm offering," Gonçalo continued. "You concur and you act at City Hall without discussing our policy in the Party. You publicly condemned the action taken at the fair with the farmers. You came to an agreement with Silva Penedo for City Hall to condemn—as they did in a statement—the Flowers Street community's struggle against the negligence that led to the disaster that hurt that young boy, who's still in the hospital."

"There are the proofs," said Pedro. "Deny them if you can. You're accusing us of precisely what you could be accused of."

The argument continued heatedly and bitterly, drawing the opinions not nearer but even further apart.

Pratas did not conceal his unhappiness. The meeting had gone badly for him. Maybe because it was Fradique, not himself, who opened the debate and led it. In the future he would have to resume taking that responsibility himself. Not bragging, but he always managed to win the arguments. At least, so he believed. This time, as Fradique had not answered Gonçalo and Pedro's conclusions, as he could and should have done, Pratas didn't respond; he stayed quiet and allowed the meeting to end as it did. For the first time, he felt dissatisfied with himself. He would learn a lesson from what had happened.

17

Around ten o'clock one Sunday morning, a group of farmers came to the Party Center. They entered, and Joana came out from the bar and led them to the office, where a few members of the District Committee could usually be found reading the newspapers.

Assuming the role of director of the Center, Pratas told them to have a seat and asked why they had come.

They explained. They came from the parish of Santa Feliciana and they had attended the latest fair here in town. The problems they were facing were getting worse. With the government's importation of potatoes, the farmers had no buyers for their substantial production.

"I myself brought this problem to the mayor," Pratas lied. "So, what do you want from us?"

"We were asleep," continued the farmer who spoke next. "It was you people who opened our eyes."

And putting his hand in his pocket, he pulled out the manifesto that had been handed out at the fair.

"What we want from your party is to tell us what we can do now."

Although aggravated, Pratas didn't lose his composure. As there were no other members of the District Committee present, he only said, "We will consider it, you can rest assured."

And rising from his chair, he indicated that the meeting with the visitors was over.

Although not satisfied, they also rose to leave. They were just exiting the room when Pedro came in and confronted them head-on. It was he who had distributed the flyer at the fair. Right away, he was recognized with visible pleasure.

18

"Hey, friends! You're not coming and going, are you? Let's all go to the bar and have a glass."

They drank and talked.

Pedro talked with them about how to find them in the parish. He insisted that they couldn't accept the situation passively. They agreed that in two weeks' time he would go to Santa Feliciana and seek out one of them, Jerónimo, whom they chose, to meet with in his home. That would continue to be the regular liaison to the Party.

Gonçalo joined Pedro, and they accompanied the visitors to the door. When they returned to the room, Vanda, who had heard the conversation, lost no time. "Will you take me with you, Pedro?"

"Sure," he answered.

Observing Pedro's engagement with the farmers, Pratas couldn't contain himself. "What kind of scheme are you going to cook up over there?"

"We'll see at our meeting," Pedro retorted.

At the meeting Pratas was very clear. He also was against the importation of potatoes, and had always said so. Now, after the visit from the farmers, he was already thinking of bringing the issue up again with Silva Penedo. But he would like to know what kind of trouble Pedro was going to stir up with the farmers.

Fradique spoke next. "I'm thinking of writing an in-depth article in the *News*, warning against taking any destabilizing actions, when the solution to problems in the district requires social peace."

"Political action, yes," Pratas commented. "Childish foolery, no."

Pedro patiently related what he had agreed with the farmers. He thought it all well and good whatever the comrades wanted to write or say condemning the importation. But the central issue was the organization and struggle of the farmers themselves and their connection to the Party. He was determined to follow through on the commitment to the farmers and go to Santa Feliciana in two weeks.

"Meaning," Pratas interrupted, "you're acting on your own decision without respecting the collective opinion?"

"No, comrade," Gonçalo jumped in. "I'm in agreement with Pedro's initiative, and we all have to help him."

"I agree," said Hermínio.

"So there we have it—the Orthodox faction in action!" Pratas yelled.

"Don't answer him, Pedro," Gonçalo cut him off. "The three of us did not meet separately to make decisions. As long as our views are in synch, we'll continue to act as you've just seen."

"As a faction, that's what it is!" Pratas insisted, rising from the table. "What do you want?" he shouted. "To impose your will?"

"No. But we will stop you from imposing yours."

"We'll see about that!" Pratas shouted again, now quite out of control. And he left, forgetting his usual custom of offering Fradique and Santos a ride home in his car.

19

On the way home, frustrated by the passion and rancor of the meeting, Pratas felt overcome by a sudden, unfamiliar sense of sadness and insecurity. A widower for seven years now, he lived with his mother-in-law and young son. Generally, when he returned home, he kissed the boy, ate what his mother-in-law had prepared for him, and shortly sat down at his desk until late, reading, writing, preparing his future speeches and commentaries with relish.

But not this night. He arrived, ate a few slices of roast beef with potatoes, though without much interest, drank a couple of glasses of wine and slowly puffed on a cigarette. "How are things going here in the house?" he asked.

There was nothing new. She had cleaned the house, gone out shopping, fixed the roast beef for lunch, ate, washed the dishes and put them away, went to visit a neighbor, returned home, drank a cup of coffee with toast, and now she was just waiting to go to bed and sleep. *How horribly boring*, Pratas thought, though most times he liked hearing her relate how her day had gone.

"And Nélinho?"

His son's day had also gone as usual. He went to school, he ate all his meals, went out to the street to play with the other boys. He'd had his dinner and now was in his room, either studying or reading or amusing himself with the Lego set his father had given him.

"Tell him to come here, if you would, please." He remained seated in his chair methodically breathing in smoke from his cigarette and lazily expelling it out his nose. The old lady brought his boy.

"Sit down," the father said. "How was your day?"
"Good."
"Good in what way?"
"Good."

"Good is not an answer, Nélinho. Okay, go to bed, it's bedtime."

The boy didn't protest and ran out of the room.

Pratas remained a few more moments at the table, unable to move. Unhappy and sorry for the way he had treated his son, he went into his room half an hour later to give him a kiss. "Sleep well, Nélinho."

He went into his office and sat at his desk. Not like his customary self, he had nothing to do, as though his usual energy had been totally sapped. He felt tired, alone, sad, discouraged—and irked and bored of all the arguments and the time he had lost on the District Committee.

20

Breaking the monotony of endless argument, a letter came to the Party Center that was nothing less than sensational. A comrade from the Regional Leadership was coming on a certain date to meet with the District Committee.

"What do they want now?" Pratas demanded. "Did someone call them?"

The man, under thirty years old, appeared on the announced date, in his shirtsleeves, and said why he had come. The problems in the district organization were well-known—an organization that seemed to be dying on the vine. The Regional Leadership had decided that he, Rodrigo, should come in and meet with the District Committee every two weeks.

"I don't understand their intention," Pratas objected. "We can solve our own problems. We don't need anyone coming from outside to teach us."

"It's not to teach, comrade. It's to help," Rodrigo calmly replied.

"What does the Regional Leadership want?" Fradique chimed in. "To subject us to Party controllers?"

"Call it what you want, comrade," Rodrigo said. "This is only a question of how the local leadership is working—"

"Control!" Pratas insisted, resuming the charge. "We can take care of ourselves!"

It was Gonçalo's turn to say something. He also wished to weigh in on the question. He considered the Regional Leadership's decision correct. There was no agreement on the District Committee. It wasn't a collective. It spent its time in interminable argumentation. Help from the Leadership was truly needed.

"No, comrades," Pratas persisted. "In the past, the leadership of lower bodies was always imposed from the top. But in our time, these bodies choose their own leaders."

"That's what the by-laws state," Fradique added.

"You're misreading the by-laws, comrade," Hermínio said. "An election or selection in lower bodies cannot contest higher leadership—that's democratic centralism."

"You mean bureaucratic centralism," Pratas corrected. "If a district needs an accountable leader, it doesn't need a comrade to come in from the Regional Leadership. It suffices for the District Committee to elect a coordinator."

And after a slight hesitation, he added, "I myself am available to assume such a responsibility, even at the sacrifice of my own personal life."

"That's all we need," Hermínio exclaimed.

"Comrade Pratas, don't play around with us," Pedro added.

Pratas's offer was not even considered.

Rodrigo again took the floor. He would relate to the Regional Leadership the initiative at the fair, the matter of the accident on Flowers Street, and the commitment that Pedro made with the farmers. The other issues could be dealt with later. This first visit was just for him to establish the connection. In two weeks he would return for another meeting with the District Committee. He ended the meeting and left.

"This business is beginning to wear me out," Pratas said to his two friends. "One of these days I'm going to put this all behind me."

21

During a break in the meeting, Joana took Gonçalo aside. She was the one responsible for the Party funds, and that week Fradique hadn't given his contribution.

As soon as the Center opened, the need arose to raise money for expenses.

Happily, the house belonged to Gonçalo's émigré brother, and already had water and electricity. Still, they needed to pay the bills. And further, they installed the bar. Besides Hermínio's offer of plates, glasses and spoons, money was needed to buy bread, cheese, ham, wine, beer and orangeade. For cleanliness and hygiene they needed to purchase a broom and dustpan, a pail, dishtowels and hand towels, and detergents.

It was the comrades of the District Committee themselves, according to each one's resources, who gave a regular contribution to cover expenses. The biggest contributors were Pratas and Hermínio. Then, Gonçalo and Fradique. The smallest were Pedro and Santos.

At first, Vanda also contributed. Part of the morning she was at the Center, and evenings and into the night she was a seamstress for Dona Leonilde. Later, as she was needed practically all the time at the Center, she was unable to continue donating, and she also no longer had income to pay for food and other personal expenses. At that point it was decided to give her a salary equivalent to what she previously had earned sewing.

"A salary?" she asked. "But the Party's funds are so limited for other things!"

She had no call to be embarrassed, Gonçalo explained. On the contrary, she should even be proud of it. The Party had functionaries, and she would be one of them.

"Me a functionary? It sounds weird and I don't like it."

But in the end she did feel the pride of which Gonçalo had spoken.

Up until the meeting that day everyone had punctually paid their contributions. Fradique not paying his was the first time that had happened.

"Should I draw it to his attention, or will you talk with him?" Joana asked Gonçalo.

"Leave it for now," he answered. "He was quite angry at the meeting. But I prefer not to believe he decided to withhold his contribution. Maybe he's had some hardship. Let it go. Let's see if he pays what he owes next week."

22

The Party Center received an unanticipated visit Sunday, from Vanda's parents, Manuel and his wife, along with their other daughter, Isabel.

They had come into town and gone to Dona Leonilde's house to see their daughters. Dona Leonilde welcomed them cordially, and Isabel enthusiastically.

"Ay, what happiness, my dear family," Isabel gushed, embracing and kissing one and all.

"And Vanda?" they asked, not seeing her at home.

Apparently they did not know yet that she wasn't living there any more and spent most of her days at the Party.

"What party?" Manuel asked, not understanding what they were talking about.

And when he learned it was a political party, and which party it was, he didn't want to believe it. It wasn't possible. Isabel surely was joking with them.

"It's true, father. I'll take you there," Isabel offered, although upset, because she also had never cared to visit her sister where she was working.

They balked. It seemed they were dreaming a bad dream.

Dona Leonilde intervened. She too hadn't liked it when Vanda made that decision. But it would be best to go there, see her and talk with her. Maybe they could persuade their daughter to go back to Dona Leonilde's house and to her work as a seamstress.

Finally they decided. They left a basket of fruit they had brought and with some annoyance, almost panic, they left with Isabel.

They entered with slow, cautious steps as though the floor were burning the soles of their feet. If it was with some shock that they went to the Party, it was with no less shock that Vanda received them.

"What? Here?" But then she came out from behind the counter and ran to embrace them.

"My dear parents! How nice! And you, Isabel, you'll never know how much I feel seeing you here."

She had them sit down at the barroom table and stood there a few moments, emotionally moved to be looking at all of them. "How nice, how nice," she repeated.

Manuel looked around. The counter, a woman behind it, some chairs, nothing more and no one else. *This is a Party? This is the Communists' headquarters?* His preconceived ideas evaporated, but still his shock and incomprehension gnawed at him.

Joana came over to join them. She offered drinks and sandwiches. No, no, they didn't want anything, they had eaten before they left for town.

On their little plot of land, they considered themselves poor. But in Manuel's eyes, what he was seeing declared a greater poverty than he had ever known.

"Is this your life?" he asked.

How could she explain it? No, she did lots of things she loved.

Manuel shook his head and said nothing more.

"Go back to Dona Leonilde's house and to your sewing, Vanda," said the mother. "I beg you, daughter, it's for your own good."

Isabel still had to lead them back to Dona Leonilde's house so they could retrieve the basket in which they'd brought the fruit.

Vanda accompanied them to the door. Her father kissed her on the forehead. Her mother hugged her, unable to hold back her tears.

Vanda stood for some time until she saw them disappear at the end of the street. She felt sadder than she had ever been before.

23

At the biweekly meeting Rodrigo reported that the Regional Leadership found Pedro's initiative concerning the parish of Santa Feliciana very positive.

He underlined that potato imports were affecting not only the farmers in the Sorzelo district, they affected producers in many other districts. It was urgent to mobilize farmers to defend their rights. In this district the struggle was very far behind, thus the importance of Pedro's establishing relations with Santa Feliciana.

Pratas disagreed. He opined that in the rural parishes the farmers were profoundly reactionary and anti-communist, the priests could lead them wherever they wanted, and there was nothing to be done with them. It was an illusion to think any differently.

"You're not right, comrade Pratas," said Gonçalo. "If we're defending the interests of the farmers, we don't ask, nor should we, if they're Catholic and if they attend mass. It's their rightful interests that we defend, and besides, it's in defending them that we will overcome anti-communist prejudices in such a way that they see in the Party their best defender. We already have that experience: their coming to the Party Center and the agreement with Pedro."

He further proposed that they take that approach as a given and that they support Pedro's initiative in Santa Feliciana.

Rodrigo broadened the discussion with new arguments and ideas.

The District Committee had an active presence only in the town. Meanwhile, Sorzelo was a medium-size district with many parishes. The District Committee up to now was no more than a local club. Not only was there much to do right in the district seat to become a truly leading organization there, but it also needed to be active outside of town in the numerous outlying parishes.

Pratas spoke up again, now in a tone that elicited surprise. In general, he said, Rodrigo's ideas seemed good. But it was necessary to gauge the actual forces at their disposition. "We here are few. We do what's possible, and even impossible for our forces. Don't ask any more of us."

Gonçalo answered. The stated objective, to go out to the parishes, constitutes a matter of vital importance. Naturally there were many difficulties facing them. What was needed was to define what they were and figure out how to overcome them.

One was the means of the District Committee comrades getting around. Another was that one or more comrades had the resources and the availability to conduct this work. Yet another was to find people to work with in the parishes.

All these difficulties were on course to be resolved.

"As we've seen, I'm ready to go," Pedro explained. "I can take off work on Sundays, which are the best days for the people there. As for transportation, we know there's no bus route to Santa Feliciana—"

"Don't count on my car for that," Pratas interrupted.

"Take it easy, comrade," Gonçalo interjected. "I'll get a bicycle from my workshop."

"Let's leave it at that," said Rodrigo. "In two weeks we'll see what's been done and how to proceed with the work."

"It's not all settled!" Pratas disagreed. "We need to see what Pedro is going to do over there. If it's—as he's already done—seeding agitation, preaching revolt, riots and social instability, the District Committee cannot agree."

"I second that," Fradique said in support.

"Me too," said Santos, after hesitating a bit.

Rodrigo took the floor again. "Comrades, the expansion of our work in the parishes is a central task. There's a comrade available. There's a means of transportation. There's the enthusiasm of the comrades. So let's move forward and we'll return to examine the issue in two weeks' time. For today, let's end the meeting."

24

Right after leaving, the esplanade three gathered on the City Hall plaza.

"There you have it—Party Control come to life," said Fradique.

"Bureaucratic centralism in action," Pratas added, once more repeating that expression. "We have to deepen the discussion. We'd better go somewhere for lunch together to refine our approach."

"I'm going home, friends. Walking. I won't be joining you today," said Santos.

"You're not coming?" Pratas was surprised.

"No, I'm going home today."

"Do you want me to give you a ride?"

"Many thanks, but I'll walk."

Fradique got into the car with Pratas and the two went on talking along the way.

"Now we're just getting the information that comes from above," Pratas said. "If it comes from above, we have to abide by it as beyond discussion. Like children obeying orders from daddy."

It could not continue like this. As he had said before, he was tired, fed up actually, with what was going on. Fradique agreed. He had already written an article about it for the *Sorzelo News*.

"An article is important. But wouldn't it be better to draft an open letter that we three would sign?" Pratas proposed. The *Sorzelo News* could play an important role. They would publish the open letter, and we shouldn't rule out getting the mass media, even radio and television to broadcast it.

25

At the same time Pratas and his friends were making their plans, Gonçalo, Pedro and Hermínio gathered in the barroom. Joana and Vanda, happy to see them together there, fixed sandwiches and served drinks—a glass of wine to Gonçalo, a beer to Pedro, and an orangeade to Hermínio.

They talked as they ate.

"I have a surprise for you today," said Gonçalo. "My wife is coming here." He had persuaded her to stop by the Center for a few minutes, for the first time. Just as he said it, his wife arrived, and Gonçalo introduced her.

Showing no bashfulness, Alice said, "Good afternoon" and effortlessly joined the conversation. "Is this your lunch?" she asked. "Gonçalo always tells me he eats well with you here at the Center." Then, in a jovial mood, she added, "It must be because you eat like this that you're all so elegant."

They liked her attitude.

"Why don't you come here more often, my friend?" Joana asked.

Alice responded with a smile. They shouldn't even think about recruiting her. She respected her husband's opinions, and respected everyone there, but a Communist she would never be.

"Why do you think that? Why say you'd never be a Communist?" Hermínio asked.

Alice let out a hearty laugh. "Because I won't!"

Not long after, with friendly words, she said goodbye and left.

Before the gathering broke up, Vanda spoke quietly to Pedro. "When we go to Santa Feliciana, how will we get there if there's no bus line?"

Pedro answered without missing a beat. "You'll have to learn to ride a bike."

He ran over to speak with Gonçalo. "For the trip to Santa Feliciana, I asked you for a bicycle, but can I get two?"

"Two? Why?"

"Vanda's going with me."

"Okay," Gonçalo agreed. "But watch out, don't crash."

26

The following night, some of the comrades encountered one another casually in the office. Pratas broke the silence. He began in an unexpected way. "The Regional Leadership wants to impose this going out to the parishes on the District Committee. Very well. We could go along with that."

He himself would be available to go to Santa Feliciana and give a speech. They just had to book a hall, promote the lecture with a flyer that they'd distribute amongst the populace, and he'd be willing to go.

"Don't mess with us, Comrade Pratas," Gonçalo cut him off. "Look, we were good enough to do all this preparatory work, we were good enough to make connections and hand out leaflets, not to develop the farmers' struggle but so that Comrade Dr. Pratas could go give a speech in Santa Feliciana. Don't even think about it, comrade."

"But what I would ask," Pratas protested, "is if there's any other comrade better qualified to go there and give a lecture. Is there anyone you might propose?"

"Party relations with Santa Feliciana are established and it's been decided," Gonçalo said, "like it or not."

"Meaning," Fradique weighed in, "you want to hold the monopoly on Party information throughout the district? And now I'm telling you, Gonçalo the bicycle man: Don't even think about it."

Pratas hadn't finished yet and expanded the range of his thinking. It was necessary in the party to put an end to vertical information: central leadership down to regional, district and parish. He had already thought through how information, and even horizontal decision-making, would be secure.

There would be no more Party Control. The District Committee would have regular contact with other district committees—in the greater Sorzelo district, for example—and together they would engage in exchanges of information and theoretical debates, and would make decisions relating to their activity.

"Total disorganization," Gonçalo broke in. Abolition of the Regional Leadership, and if the principle were applied to all regional organizations, that would signify abolition of the Central Leadership of the Party.

He rose. "We are not officially meeting here. So let's stop babbling. If these are things seriously worth discussing, it's in our Committee meeting that they should be raised." With that, he left the office.

Pratas turned to Fradique. "They want to discuss it at a meeting? Then I'll discuss it when Rodrigo comes next. I'll discuss it all calmly and insist that others do the same. But for my part, this will be the last time."

"It's time to take a stand," Fradique assented.

"Take note, Fradique. For me it's the last time."

27

Gonçalo loaned Pedro one of the two promised bicycles. Pedro left it at old Baltazar's house, and at night, leaving the Center with Vanda, they went to get it.

Old Baltazar opened the door and exclaimed ecstatically, "What a beautiful visitor you brought me, my boy. Come in, come in."

Pedro said he had only come to fetch the bicycle to teach Vanda to ride.

"Go on, then, go, children, and don't fall, girl. Any time you want to come to the house with Pedro, feel free to do so."

So Pedro began teaching Vanda how to ride a bicycle. At first it wasn't easy. More than once Pedro stopped her from falling.

He helped her find her seating and place her feet on the pedals, held onto the seat to stabilize her, pushed, increased the speed, ran, saw that Vanda was in control, let go of the bicycle, and after a few meters, seeing that she was wobbling, grabbed her and the bicycle.

They repeated the operation many times that night and the following nights. They felt a special joy being together well into the night. In a few sessions, Vanda learned.

It was one thing to learn with Pedro's help. It was something else to take command of her own bicycle and pedal ten kilometers to Santa Feliciana and back.

The first time she did it, she got such pains in her calves it was a week before she felt all right and stopped limping. But it was worth it.

Pedro and Vanda's arrival at Jerónimo's house raised and revealed attitudes and feelings that exceeded all expectations.

Piedade, Jerónimo's wife, couldn't believe it. "So young, so nice, so good-looking, and Communists? It can't be."

Jerónimo informed his wife that it was precisely those two youngsters and other friends of theirs at the Sorzelo fair who had alerted them, and clarified the issue, and who ever since had fought to defend the potato growers.

Piedade started to treat them maternally. She called her daughter, Susana, a young person like them, and told her who they were. The girl's first reaction was the same as the mother's. "Communists? It can't be."

But right away she became friendly and invited Vanda, if they were staying until the following day, to go with her to a local community dance.

"The next time," Vanda promised.

Jerónimo insisted that while the family was present, they discuss issues concerning the Party's ties with the farmers of Santa Feliciana, which they did.

The question now in the parish was how to approach organizing the struggle against importation of potatoes and make connections with other parishes.

Jerónimo had already spoken with several others in the surrounding area, and many of them were determined to act.

One more question was raised. Shortly, the festival of São Verlâncio, patron saint of the district, would take place in Sorzelo. A grand showing was being readied. They had to encourage the farmers' participation in force with their demands.

"Next time," Jerónimo said, "I'll invite a few friends I trust here to the house."

Piedade and Susana also said goodbye. "If you spend the night next time, children, I'll make sweet rice for your dinner."
"And I," said Susana, "will take Vanda to the dance."
The work in Santa Feliciana parish had begun.

28

As soon as Rodrigo arrived, Pratas took him aside. "Comrade Rodrigo, my only desire is to carry out our work. I'm going to raise some issues at our meeting. I ask that you hear what I have to say with an open mind and that we can all discuss it peaceably. I repeat, peaceably."

"That's fine—and that's how it should be," Rodrigo agreed.

Pratas began with a long oration.

There was a pressing need to correct certain undesirable situations. Without a final decision, Pedro by his own volition went to Santa Feliciana. This action did not conform to Party principles. But it's not only about this instance. Such behavior was going on every day in the name of the District Committee. He, Pratas, feared that the Regional Leadership, and Rodrigo personally, not only gave cover to such conduct, but supported it.

So this brings into relief the imperative necessity of discussing who in the end is leading our local work and who makes the decisions. If other comrades have different ideas than your own, fine. But if they act to the detriment of collective work, this is not acceptable.

Now his booming voice revealed that he had lost the peaceability he had asked for and was promised. He concluded: If the Regional Leadership gives advice, fine. But giving orders is intolerable! He, Pratas, was not prepared to accept that. And he wanted to add one more thing: He was tired of being insulted. He hid nothing of his conduct in society. He refused to keep company with the Vianas and other rich folks in the area. His relationships were with his comrades. What could they accuse him of?

No one interrupted, and almost all the comrades responded, with the notable exception of Santos, who said nothing. Fradique, in different language, recapitulated Pratas and supported his ideas. Gonçalo, Pedro and Hermínio recognized that apart from his friendship with the mayor, his social relationships were as he had said. Still, they stressed that when all was said and done, he was simply repeating ideas and opinions that had already been rejected.

"Rejected by whom?" Pratas broke in, quickly irritated—and still visibly stirred by the profession of his own impeccable social comportment.

"By the District Committee and by the Regional Leadership," Gonçalo answered.

"Was there a vote? Did anyone vote?" Pratas questioned further, almost shouting with abrasively raw, unfiltered emotion.

"We could put it to a vote, Comrade Pratas," Rodrigo suggested. "But either you'd lose, or everything would stay the same."

The Regional Leadership believed it necessary to assist the local organization and support comrades who were pursuing righteous activity. And if the impetus for Pratas's intervention was the work that had begun in Santa Feliciana, he should recall that this had been decided in a previous meeting.

"Decided?" Pratas protested. "Decided by whom?"

"Turn the disk over and it plays the same tune," Pedro murmured.

"What's decided is decided," Rodrigo affirmed calmly.

"Are you the dictator now?" Pratas bellowed, ending the meeting.

"We're done for today," Rodrigo concluded without reacting to the insult. "Until next time, comrades."

Before everyone left, Joana approached Gonçalo. "I spoke with Fradique about turning in his contribution."

"And?"

"He answered me with these words: 'It's over.'"

29

Shaken and disturbed by his own unpredictable, high emotions, Pratas returned home. Driving his car, he found the road easing his exacerbated state of mind as a gradual, vaguely defined melancholy took over. Always so combative, so self-confident, so sure of his superiority of mind and will, he now felt suddenly despondent and inert.

When he arrived home, his mother-in-law and his young son were waiting for him. He sat on the sofa and, quite unlike himself, called his son to his knees, hugged and kissed him. Nélinho took shelter in his embrace.

The mother-in-law noticed the change. "Are you all right? Did you have dinner? Shall I fix you something?"

No, he'd already eaten, Pratas responded in a subdued voice that no one in the house had ever heard.

Father and son remained quiet and still for several minutes. "It's time for bed," he said finally, placing the child on the floor and kissing him lovingly once again.

The mother-in-law said goodnight, and he remained sitting for a long time. The idea of lying down and sleeping appealed to him, not because he was sleepy, but because he was possessed by a strange apathy that clouded his consciousness and created in him an anguished need to escape reality.

Rodrigo's last words kept coming into his mind, like sharp lightning bolts piercing his brain: "It's decided." "Until next time, comrades."

The night passed, and no concrete idea emerged. He couldn't even decide to go to bed. It was dawn already when, still sitting, he fell asleep. When he woke up, the sun was high. He stood up, took a bath and shaved.

"Would you like to eat something?" his mother-in-law inquired.

"Yes, if you would, coffee and toast."

30

After the meeting, Fradique, too, returned home in a new state of mind. Not like Pratas, sad, melancholy, discouraged. But with the firm intention to act.

As always, right off he sat at the table, waiting for his wife to serve him his meal, his wrinkled face and spritely look refracted through his thick lenses. But in his manner and his words he appeared unrecognizable.

With her adorable face and angry voice, his wife greeted him petulantly, as usual. "It's late, and I waited up for you. A servant at your orders, right?" she growled as she set the table.

To her surprise, Fradique did not respond in the same timbre, but to the contrary: "My little dove, I have good news for you."

Gracinda placed what she had cooked on the table as she said, "I know you well, Fradique. I'm tired of your lies. I've told you already: This will end badly."

"You'll be pleased, but I won't share it with you today, little dove."

Having finished his dinner, he drank one more glass, and hurried into his office.

"All set!" Gracinda yelled. "There he goes, off and running. It's arrive, eat, shut himself up in his office, and not even goodnight. What a cursed life."

At the end of the Party meeting, Fradique felt the urgent need to take a position. Until long into the night he put into writing what he was thinking of showing Pratas the next day.

When he turned off the light on his desk, morning light was just dawning.

31

The following morning, Pratas did not head straight to the Party Center, nor to the esplanade for a coffee. He rambled aimlessly through the streets, leaving town on the road toward the pine forest. He was thinking hard. And in contrast to the immense fatigue that smothered him after the meeting the night before, his energy rebounded along with his thoughts.

He returned to town with a firm stride, found Fradique and Santos at the Center and proposed that they decamp to the esplanade to talk. "I want to talk with you about a very serious matter," he pronounced with uncommon composure. "I've thought, and I've decided. I've had enough—more than enough. I've thought a lot, and decided. I'm leaving the Party. As it is now, it's not for me anymore."

As an independent, he would try to do his part in the district to effect left-wing policies. And whether the others in the

Party liked it or not, a left politics in the district could only be achieved with Silva Penedo.

"I had the same idea," said Fradique. "It's time already to put an end to a situation that leads nowhere."

Pratas had also thought about ways to spread the news. They could announce their leaving the Party in an open letter, as they'd already discussed. At that time it was to publicize their position within the Party, and now it was to make public their resignation. There would be three signatures of some gravitas.

"Exactly what I was thinking," Fradique agreed. "And I've even drafted a statement to that effect."

"One moment," Santos interjected.

He understood the integrity of the other two men's decision. He would be very inclined to sign an open letter with their own views, as previously discussed. But an open letter about leaving the Party he wouldn't sign.

"What? You wouldn't sign?" Pratas exploded as if he had heard wrong.

"No, I wouldn't sign. I'm staying in the Party."

For a few moments Pratas didn't know what to say. "Then the two of us will sign, Fradique and I," he said at last. "Your signature won't be missed much."

"Do as you see best. I am staying in the Party," Santos restated.

The open letter, with the declaration of resignation from the Party by two members of the District Committee, was published in the *Sorzelo News* and cited in the mass-circulation press and on television.

At first, the reaction at the Party Center was one of indignation and dismay. But at the same time the general sentiment was that without the tumultuous arguments and conflicts, they would be in a new and better shape to do their work.

Some wondered about Santos not signing the open letter, and about his appearance at the Center as if nothing had happened as far as he was concerned. No one turned against him. To the contrary.

With the constant confrontations gone now from the District Committee, activity took on new dimensions and projects.

32

Alice showed up again at the Party Center, this time carrying huge bundles. No, she hadn't come to join the Party. The Party required a certain kind of discipline, and she preferred to keep her freedom and independence. She had come with another purpose. She not only had an opinion to offer, but an issue to resolve. A sandwich was not a lunch. She knew this very well: Sometimes, when Gonçalo came home for dinner, he ate like a wild man. The comrades needed to keep up their strength for what they were doing.

She brought a portable oil stove, a pot, a ladle, bowls and spoons, her offering to the Center. If they'd eat a hearty soup, they'd be reinvigorated.

The comrades barely knew what to say. But it was Alice, with her ready smile, who rose above their speechlessness. "Now, my friends, you'll just have to put up with me some more."

33

Gonçalo asked Pedro into the office. He needed to speak with him. Now that they were free of the unending argument and dissension, it was high time to reflect on the present situation of the Party. He was now aware of serious deficiencies, many of them in his own work. He'd like to examine these concerns together.

Lately attention had been focused on the ties to the parishes, especially Santa Feliciana. But they hadn't been giving consideration to labor in Sorzelo itself, the district seat.

"The most recent debates led me to some thinking. I'm a worker. You, Pedro, are also a worker. Our Party is a party of the working class. But we're involved in the struggle of the farmers, and we've barely looked at the possibilities, however limited, of working-class struggle, and workers in general."

"That's true," Pedro agreed. But there, in Sorzelo, where was the working class, aside from a few masons and carpenters?

"We have to own our own weakness, Pedro. There are still some workers, though only a few, in the cookie factory. There are retired people, who are also workers. What have we done to defend their interests? When and where have we ever sat down with them to formulate their demands? And you, Pedro, don't you know other masons? Now you're working in isolation on old Baltazar's wall at his house. But before, you were working on jobs with other masons. Don't you ever see any of them?"

"Only once in a while now, on the way to the Center I run into a fellow from town I used to work with, but I never thought he'd be interested in any kind of serious activity."

Gonçalo disagreed. "You don't know him well. If you talked more with him, you'd get to know him better."

The conversation went on at length, and they agreed on some lines of action. Establish contact with the few workers still employed at the cookie factory. Seek out contact with retired people and small shop owners. Also meet housewives, bringing up the issue of high prices of consumer items. Advance societal demands, the low retirement pensions, the need for a senior center. And figure out what to do about the youth.

As they talked, they gained greater consciousness of the size and complexity of such tasks, and the extreme weakness of the Party organization in the district.

"We're practically starting from zero," Pedro said frankly.

"No, Pedro. We're very few, but we're determined and we fight. The main thing, now that we've ended the constant, sterile debates and quarrels, is for us all to act collectively and with conviction."

Agreed on these ideas, they decided to call a meeting of the reconstituted District Committee: those two, Hermínio and Vanda.

"Maybe Joana could join us too."

"Agreed," said Gonçalo.

34

As planned, Pedro and Vanda went out one Sunday to hike through the leafy outskirts of town. They left by the road to Santa Feliciana, avoiding the pine forest, and cut through a path toward the fields.

The sun rose in the blue sky, warming the atmosphere without dissipating the fresh perfume of wild flora in the air.

The path opened onto a terrain tawny with dry vegetation, dotted by lush clusters of bright, shiny green trees.

As the young couple passed, the loud chirping of birds arose.

Mesmerized by nature, Pedro and Vanda proceeded in silence, sometimes holding hands, other times with Vanda holding the basket in one hand and Pedro with his arms swinging alongside his body.

Pedro broke the silence. "It'll be noon shortly. Shall we find some shade to sit in?"

Vanda peered in every direction, chose a place, and pulled Pedro with her in a run for it. "Here!"

Once they were seated, she breathed deeply, laughed, took hold of the basket, spread a cloth on the ground, and handily deployed the lunch she had brought from home: bread, fried fish, a couple of cheeses, red apples, a bottle of water, glasses and paper napkins.

All was good; it couldn't have been better. An authentic picnic. They gladly ate with the appetite of young, healthy people.

Vanda packed everything back into the basket. They were quiet a few minutes. Then the conversation started flowing spontaneously and naturally in new directions.

"You know, Pedro? We're here as friends. We get along well. But have you noticed? We barely know each other."

"That's not so," Pedro answered. They knew each other at the Center and in the work of the Center, in political life and action, and through their talks when Pedro walked her back home. And about her, he knew she and her sister had come from a family of modest means in the surrounding area to live and work at Dona Leonilde's house, the town's famous seamstress. He knew what a nice girl her sister was and how much they loved one another.

About him she knew he had come to Sorzelo with other workers and a contractor to work on some jobs at the Viana mansion. And that once the work had ended and the others went back to their hometowns, he had stayed in town to continue working.

All this had brought them together. It explained why they walked home together and at this moment were taking a stroll

through the fields. They knew each other well enough and long enough to be sincere friends.
Vanda shook her head. Pedro didn't understand her. "All that is correct, Pedro. But what more do you know about me? About my feelings? About the way I see you?"
"Little by little we'll get to know each other better," Pedro said, "and we'll keep evaluating how we feel."
Vanda laughed. "I hope so, Pedro, but you haven't understood anything I said."
She shook her head, and in a quick gesture that changed the course of the conversation, she reached out her arm and caressed his face. "Don't take what I said badly, Pedro. I'm being foolish. What I do know about you is enough to say you really are my best friend."

35

Pedro and Vanda returned to Santa Feliciana. As he had earlier proposed, Jerónimo brought together several other farmers to participate in the meeting at his house. They spoke of the protests against potato imports.

People knew that in various parishes of the district farmers were getting together to discuss the situation. They also knew from the newspapers that in other districts significant protests were emerging.

Now the task was to try to promote a large meeting of the farmers of Santa Feliciana to decide what forms of struggle to pursue to ensure their potato sales. They considered a mass demonstration in Sorzelo in front of City Hall.

At this meeting they also talked about preparations for the forthcoming Festival of São Verlâncio in Sorzelo.

Pedro and Vanda spent the night at Jerónimo's house.

Susana, Jerónimo's daughter, kept her promise. She took Vanda to the dance. The boys and girls there, apparently not knowing the reason for Vanda's trips to Santa Feliciana, liked her so much that they invited her to come visit them anytime she came to the area.

Piedade also kept her promise. At dinner she offered them sweet rice—creamy, with cinnamon and a light touch of lemon. Delicious!—like nothing they'd ever eaten.

In the morning, when they departed, everyone hugged and kissed as though they were longstanding friends. Pedro and Vanda mounted their bicycles and left.

For some reason, the return to Sorzelo was slower, as if unconsciously to prolong the trip. Passing through the pine forest, they got off their bicycles and sat on a slope.

The summer temperature was pleasant, with no breeze. The fresh air smelled of resin.

Why should they go on kidding themselves? Longtime friends they were—but only friends. Yet something different was growing between them. And before they said anything, nature came out with the truth, and love aroused the heat of their feelings and the urgency for pleasure.

They remained pressed together, mute, for a long time.

Pedro broke the silence. "I want you as my companion, not just in random outdoors encounters."

He lived with old Baltazar, who had welcomed Vanda with open arms. But would he agree to having her live there in the house as Pedro's companion?

"I'll ask him," Pedro said. "But I'm sure he'll be very happy with the idea."

He was not wrong. "Wonderful news, kids! You didn't even have to ask. It will add to our family in the house."

Dona Leonilde and Isabel didn't ask any questions. They were too upset. Only Isabel commented, "Just be careful what you're getting into."

"Don't worry. It's for my own happiness."

36

Several days later, when Pedro and Vanda returned late to the house, old Baltazar was waiting for them. Seated at the table, he put his newspaper aside. "Have a seat, kids. I want to talk with you."

Pedro and Vanda sat across from him.

"Before we start, just tell me, do you want something to eat?"

No, they had eaten.

"All right, then, listen to what I have to say. What are the people like over at the Party? Are they like you, Pedro?

And like you, Vanda? I'd like to go visit you, but I'm afraid of being disappointed. You're the only Communists I know. I'd like to see the Center, but I don't want to be disillusioned."

"Why is that, my friend?"

He had heard what happened with Dr. Pratas and Fradique the journalist, who had resigned from the Party. They made such accusations, it sounded like the Party comrades were always in open warfare and subject to dictatorship.

Pedro explained to him that the two who had resigned were the ones who sought to impose their own dictatorship. Now, in the Party, everyone was just an ordinary comrade. He should come with them to the Center and he'd be convinced. They could go over at lunchtime.

"We don't have gourmet food like you cook! But I'm not inviting you for the food. If I take you there, it's just to see what kind of people we are."

"Like you? Like your girlfriend?"

"We're all different, but we're equal."

The next day, when he'd finished the morning's work on the wall around the house, Pedro called for old Baltazar, and the two walked to the Center.

They ate a soup prepared in the pot on the oil stove that Alice had brought there.

"It was gourmet!" old Baltazar said radiantly.

He got to know Joana, and was waited on by Vanda. He also met Gonçalo and enjoyed talking with him. "I knew his name, but it was quite different meeting him in person."

"It's good that I went," he told Pedro later. "I never imagined there'd be people like that. I'd like to go back, is that possible?"

"Why not, Uncle Baltazar? You'd be welcomed as one of our own."

37

People breathed a new air at the Party Center. Everyone jumped in to help one another. The smallest tasks were completed with joy. And with frequent visitors the space no longer seemed so empty as before.

Vanda expanded her own potential. It wasn't just the visits to Santa Feliciana. It was more to do in the bar, with the stove and new cooking equipment that Gonçalo's wife had contributed. Now she was making soup, omelettes and fried eggs. She was devoted and hardworking as always. There was another thing, though, that amplified her natural high spirits. Everyone noticed it.

She had so much energy that when she had free time she went to help out her sister on the sewing jobs at Dona Leonilde's house.

It was on one of those visits to the house that she began realizing a project she'd been mulling over.

"Why do you want that fabric?" Dona Leonilde asked, seeing her place an enormous piece of red cloth on the sewing machine, and sew a hem on it.

"It's to put on the table in the bar," Vanda answered.

"It's in bad taste," Dona Leonilde couldn't resist sneering. "It's not fitting."

Her curiosity increased days later when Vanda showed up again. She used the sewing machine to quickly add pieces of yellow cloth onto the red panel. Once sewn on, she folded it and furtively placed it all in a paper bag.

"Why so mysterious?" Dona Leonilde asked.

"No, really," Isabel interjected, "where are you going to put it? I don't believe it's for the table in the bar. It would be in bad taste, as Dona Leonilde said."

"Come back to the Party some day and you'll see," Vanda answered.

Indeed, they could see—not a tablecloth in the bar, but displayed in an honored place on the wall, a red banner with the hammer and sickle in yellow.

38

Rodrigo met with the new District Committee. "Gonçalo, chair today's meeting, would you? I want to see and hear you folks conducting your work." There being no objection, Gonçalo took the floor.

He began by raising the problem of the composition of the District Committee. With Pratas and Fradique gone, it was reduced to four members. Santos attended the meetings, expressed his disagreements, but didn't join the others in the work.

The tasks were growing, and Gonçalo, Pedro and Hermínio weren't up to them all. It was necessary to enlarge the Committee.

The proposal came out of the blue: It came from Pedro. "Vanda has participated with us in all our work, such as recently in Santa Feliciana. She's as active and capable as any of us. I propose that she be named to the District Committee."

"What's extraordinary," said Hermínio, "is that we're only now considering her."

The proposal was approved.

Gonçalo then reported his progress on the tasks that had been assigned to him. He was able to contact the now retired former workers at the cookie factory. These folks were discouraged and resigned, living on reduced benefits and not engaged in any activity. A few of them got together to play cards and that was their life.

He had met with a few of them together. They spoke of insufficient pensions and the lack of a social life. He underlined the need to fight for a raise in benefits and for the establishment of a senior center in Sorzelo. They were interested in meeting again the following week.

"Did you speak in the name of the Party?' Rodrigo inquired.

No, he hadn't spoken of the Party yet, although everyone knew him as a Communist.

"Sensible," Rodrigo said quietly.

Next to speak was Pedro. It wasn't easy making connection with workers in civil construction. He had worked on certain jobs with some, but never established relationships with them outside of work. With the exception of one fellow, Daniel, whom he hadn't seen for quite some time. He knew where he lived and passed by there hoping to find him as if by chance. They went for a coffee together. He didn't do as Gonçalo did. He told the guy he was in the Party.

"And?" Hermínio asked.

"He wanted to continue talking. I told him other workers with whom I'd been on jobs expressed interest in knowing what, after all, the Communists stood for, and that I had set up a meeting with some of them."

He had invited them to the Center to have a drink. They accepted, some started coming around regularly for some healthy fellowship, and then a promising event came about that we haven't seen in a long time: Daniel signed up as a member of the Party.

As for the farmers in Santa Feliciana, things were on a solid path. He had held a meeting with a large group at Jerónimo's house. They were in a mood to fight against potato imports and to secure sales of their big crop. They demonstrated trust in the Party. Taking advantage of the Festival of São Verlâncio, they'll be coming to town in a parade of their carts with big loads of potatoes, which they'll dump in front of City Hall.

"It might not be the most correct form of struggle, but it was they who decided it and I didn't want to set the Party against them," Pedro stressed. "Afterward, they'll participate in the festival on the fairground."

Hermínio also give a report on his activity. For him it was hard to make any connection of interest with his colleagues at the business where he worked. They were technical bureaucrats who didn't want to know about anything except fancy eating, the high life and trivial things. There was nothing he could do there. But he did take seriously his assignment of buying and reading newspapers, selecting and cutting out news of concern to the Center's work. He had the clippings with him that he'd make available in the office.

"Vanda, you're last," Gonçalo said.

She spoke in the same natural manner in which she always spoke. The most regular and interesting assignment she had was in the Santa Feliciana parish. She went there with Pedro. Pedro met with the farmers and she was brought by Jerónimo's daughter to visit some local association projects. She was well received, and both the daughter and the other girls welcomed her without reservation. On the last visit to the parish, she agreed with a group of girls to organize an excursion to Sorzelo.

"That's all, comrades," she concluded.

Gonçalo asked if Rodrigo wanted to add anything.

"Go on, go on," he limited himself by way of response.

Gonçalo then proposed to examine the issues the comrades brought up, which they did. They suggested new steps to take to further the work already done. And Gonçalo summarized the conclusions.

At that point Rodrigo took the floor. "The District Committee, comrades, is proceeding nicely on its own two feet and on its own initiative. You can close the meeting, Gonçalo."

"Good, comrades," Gonçalo said, "that's it for today. We'll expect Comrade Rodrigo back in two weeks."

"Wait, wait! I won't be here in two weeks. The Regional Leadership has a lot to do in other areas. You all are pursuing your work quite well. I'll return here a month from now."

39

On the eve of the Festival of São Verlâncio, the Center was a hub of activity preparing the Party's table.

Everyone was there: Gonçalo, Pedro, Vanda, Hermínio, Joana, Santos and Daniel, and also non-Party members, Gonçalo's wife Alice and old Baltazar.

They were debating the sign to attach to the table.

"Party of the farmers," Daniel suggested, enthused as he was by the news that they were coming in force from Santa Feliciana.

"That won't work, friend," said Gonçalo, giving his opinion. "Our Party is the party of the working class, so that slogan on the sign would be out of place. Let's hear some other suggestions."

Several others came, and it was old Baltazar who came up with an idea that led to the final choice. "Maybe 'Party of all the people.' What do you think?"

"Good idea," Pedro approved. "With a slight change it might be better: 'PCP, always with the people.'"

It was approved, passed and done.

"I'll design the letters," Hermínio offered.

"And Vanda and I will paint the sign," Joana added.

In an instant, Joana and Vanda spread a white cloth of the required dimensions on the floor, and with brushes and paints sat themselves down on the floor to start working.

At the table, Alice had brought red and green silk paper, rolls of wire and pliers. They would make a good quantity of paper carnations—the democratic symbol of the 1974 Revolution. Alice commandeered the operations, showed how to make the carnations and corrected mistakes. Gonçalo cut pieces of wire and handed them to the others. Although slow, Santos did his work with gusto. Pedro and Daniel, unrestrained, competed to see who could make the most. Old Baltazar also happily competed and each time he finished a little flower, he held up his arm to show it off to the others before dropping it into the basket where they piled up.

"If you wind up unemployed," Pedro joked to Daniel, "now you have a new profession."

Meanwhile, Hermínio on the floor was designing the panel with beautiful lettering: "PCP, always with the people."

When Joana handed over the paint, Vanda let out a cry: "Blue? No way, Joana. At least 'PCP' has to be in red."

"But blue is pretty," Joana insisted.

"All right, then," Vanda conceded. "Let's paint 'PCP' in red and the other lettering in blue. But underlining the blue with red."

Now in accord, they launched into their work. Those two on the floor, the others at the table making paper carnations, they all wanted to see who would finish their work first.

"Done!"—it was Joana who was first to shout victory.

"Wait!" Vanda yelled. "We have to paint a hammer and sickle."

At the table they finished their job: a basketful of paper carnations. They rose and went to the counter at the bar, where Joana and Vanda served drinks. They got ready to leave.

"Listen, comrades," Vanda said. "I bought a few red carnations. I want to put one on my lapel. Who else wants one?"

They all did.

They exited the door together and only when they got to the street separated to go their own way—Hermínio with Joana, Gonçalo with Alice, Pedro with Vanda and old Baltazar. For a few moments Daniel was standing alone.

"Come along with us as far as you like," Pedro told him. "We won't let you leave here by yourself."

40

Sorzelo celebrated its patron saint, São Verlâncio.

In the morning, as every year, there was mass at the church, a mass like any other mass. The priest preached gratitude to the patron saint for the faith of the believers, for everyone's protection against misfortune, and for their daily bread.

Following, at City Hall, was a solemn session with more chairs empty than occupied. Dr. Pratas and Fradique attended, along with other distinguished persons of the district. Elusive as ever, the Vianas did not deign to appear.

Silva Penedo held forth. He spoke at length about the patron saint in the history of the district. He said little of interest but received the polite applause expected on such occasions.

When the session ended, the participants left City Hall and went their different ways, some by car, others on foot. On the other side of the square, the café on the esplanade was full as usual. But with the grand popular festival occurring at the fairground, the square seemed deserted.

The mayor came out of City Hall, got into his blue car and left, to a slight flurry of interest on the esplanade.

"You have to recognize," said Fradique, "the car befits the office he occupies."

Resignation from the Party and the open letter did not accord its two signatories any greater prestige or authority. To the contrary. That afternoon, one of the other customers on the esplanade, seated at a table next to Pratas and Fradique, daringly asked, "Excuse me, Doctor Pratas, why are you wearing a yellow carnation in your lapel?"

Pratas was struck dumb. But finally he came up with an explanation. "It's a sign of independence," he responded superciliously.

"Aaaah!" his interrogator exclaimed.

Around noon, the cortege of carts from Santa Feliciana arrived at the plaza. To the visible shock of everyone on the esplanade, they unloaded their carts in front of City Hall. The square was carpeted with potatoes. Many of them rolled out, reaching the café customers' feet.

"Yet another smartass joke from *the comrades*," Fradique snorted as he rose from his chair and looked out over the square.

Meanwhile, on the vast fairground, the festival was taking place.

The townspeople showed up in force, as well as people from several surrounding parishes. Vendors set up little stands to sell wine. As their barrels emptied, the appetizing smell of roasted meat spread through the air, from a calf the Festival Committee had purchased for the day.

The retired seniors, under an awning offering protection from the sun, were conversing excitedly. Their sign read, "We want a Senior Center."

At their stall, the farmers of Santa Feliciana displayed another sign: "We demand an end to potato imports."

Some unknown fellow appeared to liven up the festival with the seductive sound of his accordion. Seated on a bench by himself, he played popular songs. It was his offering, and he asked nothing in exchange.

At their little table, the Party newspaper was on sale, alongside the silk paper carnations. Gonçalo, Pedro, Vanda, Hermínio, Joana and Daniel were there, with red carnations on their lapels, talking with each other and anyone who stopped by to chat. The sign on their stand read, "PCP, always with the people."

Manuel and his wife, joined by Isabel, came to the festival, and Vanda presented them with three paper carnations.

In the midst of the excitement, a boy approached the table and stopped, obviously attracted to Vanda.

"Do you want the newspaper?" she asked.

The boy hesitated. Then he spoke. "Don't you have a red carnation to sell me?"

Vanda held out a paper carnation. "I'll give you one," she offered.

"Not one of those," the boy said. "I want a real red carnation like the one on your lapel."

How could she say no? "Here, I'll give you mine," she smiled and extended her hand. He took it and placed it in a buttonhole of his shirt.

The accordion player tirelessly filled the broad festival grounds with the sweet background sound to all the other noise, the melodious harmonies of popular music.

Never had Sorzelo seen a festival like that one.

"Happy?" Pedro asked into Vanda's ear.

"Of course!" she grinned.

Délinha

TO this day, as I remember it, I can hardly believe all that happened. They were the most terrifying events of my entire life. For a long time afterward, when I woke up in the morning, I remembered what had happened and I lay there wondering if it had been a horrible nightmare. But no. All of it actually happened.

One summer I had gone for treatment to the hot springs at Vale. There were also many couples with children at the spa—lots of children, among them Délinha, so pretty that anyone who laid eyes on her would feel captivated with enchantment. I had never seen a child so beautiful.

She was six years old, with braids tied on top of her head with a little bow, a cute, rosy-cheeked face, and a permanently expressive face. Always playful, she would find some way with everyone to mimic and have fun—truly a joyful creature.

The hot springs of Vale were situated on the slope of a mountain. It was common to organize excursions for the summer visitors at the resort. That's what happened one Sunday after lunch.

Délinha's parents couldn't go on the hike as they were expecting friends who would be arriving soon for a visit. But Délinha insisted she wanted to go by herself. She was so eager to go because many other kids would also be going.

"No, daughter, since we're not going, you also can't go," her father told her. "You're being very uncooperative, child."

But Délinha kept asking, and she was so charming about it that it was hard to refuse her.

"I'll take responsibility for her," I offered. "You can trust me. She'll be very careful, isn't that right, Délinha? And if you leave her with me I won't let her out of my sight."

They gave in. And I joined the group of summer hikers, Délinha at my side.

Happily, we mounted the slope. At the top, indicated by a white stone geodesic bench mark, the view was dazzling. The energetic children accompanied the adults with delight. The grownups contemplated the panorama, and the children played.

I didn't lose sight of her. From time to time I'd look over to see that she hadn't fallen and hurt herself.

We stayed up at the top only a short while. Then we started our descent, the adults walking swiftly, the children running with excitement.

It happened as we got down to the first shoulder of the hillside. How was it possible? Where was my good sense when it happened? But it happened.

I looked all around and I didn't see Délinha. I just didn't. The other kids were there, and everyone else, but she wasn't.

"Délinha! Délinha!" I called out in every direction, without response.

She gave no response at all. She wasn't with us. The fact is, she had disappeared.

Like a madman I ran back up the incline, all the way up to the top, to make sure she hadn't fallen without anyone noticing. Nothing.

At that point we all got together to search for her, calling and shouting everywhere. Délinha did not appear.

Maybe she'd gone and hidden herself without anyone seeing. Maybe she'd got lost and couldn't find her way back. But no one, neither the adults nor the children, had seen her straying from the group. Some of the adults kept looking for her, but the group couldn't stay there forever with the kids already showing signs of fatigue.

One young man offered to stay with me and keep searching. For sure, she couldn't be very far, and in the end we'd find her. "We'll stay, then. Tell her parents that as soon as we find her we'll come right back to the spa with her."

The group left, disappearing from view as they went back down the mountain. Remaining there alone with the other fellow, I felt possessed by even greater nervousness, almost panic.

We had to search a little farther away.

The two of us who remained split off in two directions and agreed to come back to the same spot in half an hour. Certainly one of us would have found Délinha.

It was awful being alone at that moment. I had forebodings of an accident, and even a fatality. Half-crazed, I launched into a mad sprint hunting for her.

Crossing the terrain, I came upon a little isolated cabin. I ran to it and looked through the door asking if they had seen Délinha. How horrible! A child threw himself at me wanting to beat me with a stick. A woman began shouting, "Get away! Get away!"

The child was also yelling, and persisted in trying to attack me.

I had to see if by chance Délinha was there. Maybe they had kidnapped her? With two shoves, I pushed both the woman and the child aside and entered the house. It was a tiny room. I shouted for Délinha and ran to every corner of the structure. Délinha was not there.

"Out! Out!" the woman continued shouting.

I desperately looked around, searching under little cavities, behind rocks, under small shrubs. Nothing. Délinha had disappeared.

I returned to the site where I'd agreed to meet up with the other young man. He was there. He had also looked all around, without success.

People would need to come from the resort to help us find her, to beat the bushes throughout the area where she had disappeared, but now in an even wider arc. Who knows if someone had kidnapped her? This turned into an obsession for me.

"Go ask for people to help. I'll stay here," I proposed.

He left down the hill and I stayed by myself looking everywhere I could in a mad rush.

The vastness of space high up the mountain, the still air and the silence intensified the unbearable anguish I felt all alone and increased the futility of my screams.

I expanded the field of my search. Délinha had to be somewhere. Maybe she got separated and lost, and not having found the way back, wandered even farther off course. And maybe someone took off with her. It wouldn't be the only time something like that had happened. I ran through the mountains shouting her name.

Suddenly a hope arose. In one fold of the earth I heard distant singing. I ran in that direction. I came across another rise in the mountains and at its base I saw a little amphitheater with young people singing. Hope at last! Maybe she was there with them.

"Délinha! Délinha!" I yelled.

The surprised youths ceased their singing.

"Délinha! Délinha!" I continued calling.

And I heard a voice: "The guy is nuts." And hysterical laughter.

I left there confused. I never thought I had enough strength to run so many kilometers out of breath and with such a strong pain in my chest. But it was impossible to stop, impossible to return to the hot springs without the girl. Impossible, completely impossible, to stand before the parents without the daughter they had entrusted to me. And if I didn't find her, I had only one of two solutions: either allow myself to disappear with no return into some hidden redoubt on the mountain, or kill myself. Yes, kill myself. The idea came to me and repeated itself every time I shouted for her and received no answer.

I went on through the mountains, lost, my throat raw from shouting the girl's name.

So tired I could hardly drag my legs, I heard the clamor of voices from a certain distance also shouting. Surely they were the reinforcements helping with the search that other guy went to ask for at the spa. They were calling for someone. I wanted to flee. Certainly they'd come from the hot springs to help with the search. Délinha's parents must have come with them. They were calling my name. But I couldn't face them. Never. I tried to escape, but my extreme fatigue wouldn't let me.

I didn't manage to escape them. As they approached, I saw Délinha's parents in the group. They surrounded me, and it was the father who stood right in front of me. "She turned up! She's there!" he yelled.

I can't explain what came over me. I'm a person of great self-control. But I remember that I started to sob convulsively, and I was still weeping when we got back to the resort.

Délinha's parents were very generous: They tried to calm me down on the way back. On the descent from the mountain, Délinha decided she wanted to get back to the spa before all the others, and she went off on her own, running down the mountain to hug her parents at the resort, triumphant in her feat.

Surely she knew I would stay up on the mountain looking for her. When she saw me coming she drew closer with slow steps, so cute, so pretty with her little braids tied with a bow atop her crown, and made a caressing gesture on my face. I took hold of her little hand.

"I'm sorry, Délinha," I whimpered, emotionally spent.

She laughed, caressed my face once again and, escaping to her parents' side, she turned around once more and smiled.

Lives

The Apportionment

THE father summoned his two sons. He wished to talk with them. Silvino and Amadeu were robust young men who, even as children, worked with their father on the family's small farm.

They also had a little food market. The produce from the farm supplied the house and helped balance the books, but it was not very profitable. The father was a benevolent man: He sold on credit and forgave the poor people who owed him.

The farm provided enough to keep the house running. There was a lovely kitchen garden, a little orchard, chicken coop and rabbit hutch. That is, vegetables, fruits, eggs and meat. And they managed.

But that wasn't a future for the boys, said the father. He had thought it over. He'd like to have enough resources to send both of them off to study and prepare for a career. But what he had wouldn't be enough for that. And even if he had it to give, if both of them left the area for their studies, how would he look after the farm by himself? He had pondered it deeply and had a solution to propose.

"One of you can stay with the farm and the store, and the other can follow a course of study, maybe go to veterinary school."

"I don't have the brains for studies," Silvino replied. "And I don't mind if Amadeu goes."

"If that's what Father wants to do," said Amadeu, "well, it would be a dream come true for me to go study."

"Think hard about it, sons. I trust there won't be any misunderstandings between you on account of this apportionment. That you, Silvino, won't come to regret not going to study, and that you, Amadeu, don't regret not staying with the market and the farm."

Not at all. They were both good friends with each other, they respected the decision, and under any circumstances they would help one another, and Father as well.

"May it be so, my sons. May it be so. And may God help you all through your lives."

The Brief, Romantic Love Between Amadeu and Glória

Amadeu enjoyed much success in his studies at the veterinary college. He learned how to treat cattle and horses. With his diploma in hand, he headed off to the Almar district of Alentejo. It was a region of huge latifundias across immense plains, bordering on the Manso River. They produced rice and other grains, cork, black pigs in the oak groves, cattle and horses.

People in the region spoke much of one young woman's fortune, Glória by name, already well-known as Dona Glória. She was the sole inheritor of the extensive latifundias known as House of Cedars, whose owners—her parents—had been killed in a traffic accident.

Amadeu didn't lack for work. He was called upon by wealthy property owners. But for some time he had not received a call from House of Cedars. Until one day, when it happened.

"Senhor Amadeu, the lady from House of Cedars would like you to come and treat one of her horses."

Amadeu attended the horse. It had a deep wound on its leg. Several times, Glória stopped in to observe the treatment. Amadeu was a handsome young man of a friendly nature. Over the years, Glória had refused several rich suitors, but she felt lonely. To the surprise of her staff at House of Cedars, his visits to see the horse turned into visits to see the senhora. It ended, to even greater shock, with a private marriage sanctified by the bishop of the district who was a regular visitor at the House.

Their honeymoon was very intimate: They lived together and got to know each other with mutual, unassuming enchantment. Their whole future was ahead of them. They were absolutely sure, as they said to one another, they would live this enchanted life for many years to come.

Fate declared it not to be, and their happiness did not last long. One night Amadeu awoke with violent shaking, his teeth shivering from the relentless cold. In those times malaria victimized many people in the rice-growing areas. The doctor was of no use, and Amadeu died of a high fever a few days later.

Glória wore black from then on, never any other color. She wept copiously over the loss of her first, and it would be her only, love in life.

When the pain softened, she told Silvino about the death of his brother, offering help as needed to him and his family.

The years passed. Her own sorrow led her to understand and feel the pain of others. Dona Glória became a generous benefactor. She made donations to several poor families and for charitable works. She sent contributions for the prisoners to have a nice Christmas. She became known as a person who loved her neighbor.

By contrast with this spirit given over to charity, her character evolved and was further defined: She had an iron will in her decisions. At House of Cedars it was she and she alone who ruled.

And if years later she wound up accepting one of two daughters of one of her brothers, who had passed away a long time before, as a resident at House of Cedars, it was more an act of charity than an obligation. Twenty years younger than Glória, Carlota went to live at House of Cedars like an adoptive daughter. But every decision continued to be the entire and sole prerogative of Dona Glória.

Silvino and His Children

Silvino's life ran its course. A few years after Amadeu left for his veterinary studies, Silvino married Cremilde, a poor girl from a neighboring town. In due time came the children—two boys, João and José, and two girls, Rosário and Cristina.

While Amadeu was at school, Silvino and his father supported the raft of kids. After a few years, Father weakened, got sick and, feeling death near, called his son.

"Silvino, my son, I'm going to leave you. It's too much for you to work and sustain your numerous family. Write to Dona Glória. She promised to help you. The time has come for it."

After Father died, Silvino endured working all alone for some years. It's hard to understand where he got the fortitude for it. True, Cremilde did help out in the market, apart from her household chores and looking after the children. And it's also true that the older son João and José did start making important contributions toward the family enterprise. Even as children, they helped their father on the farm, and their mother on the market and taking care of the younger ones. Being the oldest, and because of his extraordinary energy, João began acting like the future head of the family. It became almost impossible to feed so many mouths. But it wasn't only food. It was clothes and shoes, medicine when they were sick, the thousand and one expenses of a large family.

Silvino wrote to Dona Glória, letting her know about their situation. And, keeping her promise at the time of Amadeu's death, Dona Glória offered to help them, even generously. She was prepared to receive Rosário and Cristina at House of Cedars when they reached adolescence. And immediately she would give a scholarship to João or to José so that, similar to what occurred with Amadeu, one of them could go and take a course of study.

Silvino placed before his sons the same choice that his own father had put before himself and Amadeu. João wanted to stay with the farm and the market.

José left for the city with Dona Glória's scholarship.

José's Schooling and Marriage

Just like Amadeu, José also excelled in his studies. He went through secondary school rapidly and entered the university. Every year, after he successfully passed all his exams, he returned home to help out his father and João with the farm work. He assisted his mother at the market, and helped his sisters to learn to read and write. He returned to the city revived by the love for his family.

He committed one grave mistake, however. As a student, he felt lonely in the city. He met Mariana, his neighbor, and ended up marrying her and going to live with her at her long-widowed mother's house.

Dona Glória did not appreciate that he had made such a big life decision without saying anything to her. She had it in mind to find a rich heiress for him to marry, and she would not forgive him. Angry with him, she cut him off from his monthly subsidy.

At that point life got very hard for José. Living with his wife at his mother-in-law's house, the latter didn't haggle with him over his daily meals. But he needed to earn something for household expenses and for his matriculation fees, books clothes, shoes, and personal items of his toilette. Accustomed to the hardest kind of work back home, he courageously set out, though with little success, to find any kind of job, however lowly, that fit his schedule at the university. He wound up going to the train station every night unloading passengers' luggage and transporting it to their front door.

A classmate who saw him doing that kind of work couldn't believe it. "You here?"

"What of it?"—the only response he could offer.

At his house, they insisted he give up such work and dedicate himself only to his studies. He did not agree. Life went on like that for José, and in time his course of study ended.

All those years he had no connection whatsoever with Dona Glória, and she never once inquired after him. Only when he went back home to the farm did he learn that the girls were waiting to get just a little older so they could go live at House of Cedars, cordially welcomed by Dona Glória.

The Teacher José

When he finished his studies, José secured a position as a teacher in a private school, teaching 13- and 14-year-old boys in the first cycle. He held a chair in history. He taught the history of Portugal not according to monarchies, though mentioning the names of some of the kings who, by the role they played in a particular time, marked a stage of history. He demonstrated a way of teaching that took into account the interests and inclinations of his students. He taught the history of Portugal with attention to social classes and their conflicts, the changes and advances in society, and the work of writers and poets.

"This isn't in the books we have," the students complained at first.

"Of course not," he answered. "That's why I will explain it, and you'll take notes."

The school principal had his doubts about such methods and such teaching, but since the students applied themselves and got good results on their tests, he came to accept the teacher's approach.

It wasn't only the teaching of history, however, that piqued the principal's surprise and discomfort. Another aspect of José's behavior was his way of engaging with the students outside of class. He went with them to the athletic field, sat down with them on the grass and talked with them, ignoring the differences in age and status, responding to a thousand and one questions they asked him on any number of issues.

One day the principal asked him to come to his office. He wanted to draw his attention to the trust he placed in the boys and the conversations he was having with them. It seemed like he didn't know them very well, and he singled out one in particular.

Tomaz was behind in his studies, a troublemaker who took advantage of his age and size to beat on his schoolmates. The worst of it, the principal informed José, was that the other boys complained that he robbed them of things, including money. Considering Tomaz suspect, the principal said, "Doctor,"—out of respect for his university degree—"you should watch him and see if you can catch him in one of these acts. As soon as you uncover something, tell me immediately. I do not want thieves here at the school."

"No, Senhor Principal," José responded. "I'm here to teach and help. Not to play policeman. One thing I can tell you is that I am helping Tomaz and will continue to do so through all his problems."

The principal did not care for that answer, but left it at that.

In his classes, José presented his material as he strolled through the room, circulating among the desks. One time, he passed by Tomaz and saw him quickly hiding something.

"Hand it over," he said in a low voice.

The boy acted as though he hadn't heard.

"Hand it over!"

The boy gave it to him. It was a change purse. José placed it in his pocket without saying anything and continued ambling through the room explaining his lesson.

"Are you telling the principal?" Tomaz asked him.

José didn't answer. A few days later he took Tomaz aside. "Here, take it," he said, handing the purse back. "Replace the money you took out and put it back in the pocket of the classmate you took it from."

The next day, he asked, "Did you do it?"

Tomaz nodded yes.

"Don't do it again. Agreed?"

Once again, Tomaz nodded yes.

A few days later, he spoke with him again. "I have a proposal for you. You're behind in your studies. But you're not lacking in intelligence. It's possible you can recoup the years you've lost."

"How?" Tomaz asked, believing the teacher was just going to tell him he should study more to pass the third year of the first cycle.

"You are a bright young man, and with my help you could get through the second-cycle years in only one year."

Tomaz couldn't hold back his laughter. The teacher wasn't joking with him?

"I'm serious, Tomaz, if you seriously apply yourself to your studies, you'll be able to do it. I'll help you and prepare you. All right?"

Tomaz kept silent for some minutes.

"All right?" José repeated.

As if it were a matter of some new trick, half serious, half joking, Tomaz finally accepted the proposal. "All right!"

And in fact, despite the principal's doubts and reservations, with the teacher's help day after day, he studied well, took his exam and passed.

They could hardly believe it at the school. Overcoming his shock, the principal congratulated the teacher. Any way you looked at it, the student's success could be counted as the school's success.

In that way, José continued to be respected and appreciated by the students at the school.

At home, with Mariana and the mother-in-law, life proceeded as usual.

Mariana's Mother

Mariana's mother had a family history full of memorable incidents. She came from the well-known Ferreirinha family, originating in Beira. One of her ancestors died under tragic circumstances during the Liberal Wars in the 1830s. He was a Miguelista, a conservative absolutist, and when the side he was fighting on was defeated, he managed to escape. He assaulted the driver of an oxcart loaded with straw, demanding that he be allowed to hide under the straw, threatening to kill him if he betrayed him.

The story went that he hid, but on the way liberal soldiers forced the oxcart to stop, asking, "Did you see Ferreirinha? Do you know where he is?"

"He didn't pass through here," said the driver, pointing to his shirt cuff. It was impossible to know if he chose to respond that way to defend Ferreirinha and absolve himself of the lie, or if he wanted with that gesture to indicate something to the soldiers.

The soldiers interpreted the gesture in this second sense, and pierced the straw violently and repeatedly with their long bayonets. And that's how Mariana's ancestor died.

For her own part, the mother had an especially dramatic personal life. With his tiny income that could barely sustain them, her husband decided to emigrate to Brazil to try his luck. He returned poor and sick, and died soon after.

With her own small income, she went on living. She was an even-keeled, amusing lady who had a talking crow in her house. She had taught it so that whenever she was frying anything, hearing the sound, the crow asked, "Egg? Fried?"
And that made her laugh.

José's Son Xaquim

Everything ran smoothly in the house, except for the worries over the son who had been born in the meantime. A darling baby, he was a nonstop crier. He'd wake up crying and wailing in the middle of the night, and only after rocking him on your lap, walking back and forth with him, and singing to him, would he go back to sleep.

A fussy baby, always antsy and impatient, he grew, and when he started to walk, right away he wanted to scurry around the house from one corner to the other, falling, getting up again, mixing into everything, and crying and yelling whenever he did something foolish.

When he went to nursery school, the teachers always had some complaints about him to convey to his parents. Still, however unbearable, he was an adorably cute little boy.

Baptized Joaquim, it was the name he was called by throughout his infancy. But with some irritation he would would always correct: "Xaquim! Xaquim!"

And if the other kids didn't comply, Xaquim turned on them like a wild monkey and hit them so hard they would run away, half shocked, half amused.

He would stand there like a conqueror, handsome and smiling, a naughty child, but so captivating. The teachers complained to his parents. But at the end of the day, they found him amusing, hugged him closely, kissed him and laughed together.

João and His Sisters

João remained on the land continuing the life of his forebears. Silvino didn't last many more years. With each passing season, João showed himself incapable of keeping up with the work on the farm and in the market. When he returned home at the end of the year, José helped as much as he could. But the responsibility was too great for João to sustain. He decided to do what his father never even dared to think. He leased out the land to a sharecropper for a third of the land's yield, and kept just the market. And, unlike his father, he made his purchasers pay up, becoming the biggest grocer in town.

Even so, it's hard to understand how he managed to meet the needs of his sisters Rosário and Cristina for so many years. He deserved much credit.

And when they grew to adolescence and left to be welcomed in by Dona Glória, they said goodbye to their brother as though he were their second father.

Rosário, Cristina and Dona Glória at House of Cedars

As promised, Rosário at fourteen, and Cristina at sixteen, went to live with Dona Glória at House of Cedars, invited in as family members.

"You'll be like my nieces," Dona Glória told them, "and you will be treated like nieces."

And so it was. They had a comfortable room for the two of them, meals at the table with their adoptive aunt, and modest, but good quality clothes.

"If you need anything," Dona Glória reminded them, "Tell me. Since you arrived you've been treated not as my adoptive nieces-by-marriage, but as real nieces."

So it appeared. But over the long years that followed, something almost imperceptible in the manners and familiarity with which the servants treated them suggested that they were living there as relations, yes, but as poor relations in the house of a rich aunt.

The contrast became clearer compared to the treatment of Dona Carlota, the niece of the mistress of the house. A few years older than the two protected newcomers, Carlota enjoyed special privileges—a fancy bedroom, with furniture she had personally ordered, expensive, showy clothes, and the authority to boss the servants around. She was the heiress who had installed herself in the house in anticipation of the foreseeable course of life when she would become its owner.

The years passed. Yesterday, adolescents. Then, finished women.

From the start Dona Carlota looked askance at the arrival of the two sisters at House of Cedars. She did not dare to show it, however, to her aunt's face. Right from the beginning she reinforced the distinction. While the two sisters referred to her as Dona Carlota, she in turn called them simply and familiarly by their first names. In front of Dona Glória she showed a kind of attentiveness toward them, assuming even a protective attitude. She withheld what she truly felt, knowing that Dona Glória would not tolerate her willfulness.

Something happened one time that showed her once and for all how things stood.

They were all eating together in the dining room, Dona Glória at the head of the table, Dona Carlota at her right, the two sisters on the left. The service was always made in the same order: Dona Glória, Dona Carlota, Rosário and Cristina.

That time, however, the maid who was serving the table, by mistake or on purpose, switched the order: She served the two sisters before Dona Carlota.

As if calling the maid to attention, Carlota started tapping her silverware on her plate with loud, rhythmic beats, but when her aunt gave her a quick admonishing glance, she stopped.

Later, away from the table, Carlota tried to set things straight in the order she believed correct. She went into the kitchen and found the maid at fault. And before the whole staff, she chewed her out in angry tones: "Don't ever do what you did again, do you hear? If you do it again, I'm telling you right now, you'll go straight out onto the street!"

"But—" the maid tried to explain.

"Are you listening?" Dona Carlota interrupted stridently. "I repeat: Straight out to the street!"

Intimidated and hurt, the maid cried pitifully. Later, when she had calmed down, she summoned up her courage and, with a thousand pardons for serving the table out of order, she told the mistress what happened.

"Don't make that mistake again when you serve the table," Dona Glória warned.

She called for Dona Carlota and told her to sit down. "I want you to keep in mind three things I'm going to say to you, Carlota. One is that Rosário and Cristina are in this house as my adoptive nieces. Second, I do not want to create any scenes with the servants. Finally, here in this house I am the only person who can fire anyone. I do not give you authority for that."

"Someone must have given you some wrong information, Aunt—" Dona Carlota tried to justify herself.

"Shut up!" Dona Glória cut her off, raising her voice. "I do not wish to hear anything more about this. And you had better pay attention to what I have just told you. Pay close attention."

Joaquim and His Adventures

Years passed, and Joaquim, little Xaquim, continued to cause worry.

A truant at school, he flunked out several times. In a few days, the pocket money his father gave him for the whole month slipped through his fingers. When the situation got impossible, the father got work for him, but he soon left the job. He bummed around, and when he returned home without saying where he had been, he asked for his father's pardon.

"It's okay, father, I won't do that again."

"No, Joaquim, you have to learn to work and support yourself. I got a job for you in Angola. You'll go there, and you'll earn enough to live. But if you fail at that and you start being a bum again, you won't find anyone there or here to help you."

"Take it easy, father," Joaquim promised, inwardly excited about what looked like a new adventure.

Off he went to Africa, and for a long time there was no news of him. He never told his family anything about his life there. But friends who knew him there later recounted tales of his strange behavior.

On the one hand, at work he was an obedient employee. On the other hand, outside of work, he went out carousing every night, placing preposterous bets that he seemed sure to lose, but which he often won.

The family later learned that one night he made an extraordinary wager. He bet that if he were taken at night, blindfolded, some twenty kilometers from the city, and deposited in the middle of the jungle infested with wild animals, he'd be able to orient himself and return to the city.

His companions, as crazy as he was, accepted this brave bet, and according to its terms, picked up their rifles just in case, put him into a car, left him unarmed and blindfolded in the middle of the jungle, and returned to the city.

On the way back they started having second thoughts. Joaquim was running the risk, above all not knowing where he was, of getting lost, losing his sense of direction and remaining there subject to the dangers of the wild without being able to return. So they went back to the place they left him. They called out loudly, and for several hours searched for him in the area. When it got dark, they made signals with their flashlights, and only in the early morning returned to the city feeling the true weight of the crime they had committed, thinking of going back there with some natives who knew the land.

To their shock, when they got back to the city, Joaquim was already there waiting for them on the road. He didn't explain how he had escaped, but he pocketed his winnings and enjoyed a good laugh. All this, again, was learned only much later.

Riding on this and other adventures, he survived. And not even once, while he was in Africa, did he communicate with his family.

One day he came back to Portugal and reappeared in his father's house, with his usual impudence.

"As you see, father, all went well. I worked like a slave. I learned a lot. I brought a few coins back. Now I ask if you can set me up in a good job here. You can rely on me to be a good worker."

José Visits House of Cedars

More years went by. Dona Glória ended up forgiving José for marrying and making his own life contrary to her wishes and plans, while he was still a student and living on her subsidy. She wrote to João, who had earlier given her notice of the death of his father Silvino. "Tell your brother that I've forgiven him," she wrote. "Tell him I'd like him to visit me."

João wrote to José, relaying the invitation, and one Sunday, by arrangement, José came to House of Cedars.

José and his sisters had not seen each other since he, then still a student, had come back to the farm where they, still adolescents, were living. It was a reencounter of great tenderness and pain. As they eyed him, they were surprised by his streaks of white hair. And he had some difficulty recognizing in the two mature women, with somber clothing and sad expressions, the youthful faces he had last seen so many years before. Tears did not flow from eyes, but there was a catch in their voices from the emotion.

José was not expecting from Dona Glória the reception she extended. Quite aged now, and supporting herself on a cane with a silver knob, she welcomed him with full honors. She did not refer to José's marriage, which led her to cut off his grant. But she received him as though he were on a ceremonial visit. She invited him to a luncheon in a room of dark furniture and racks of display plates. She had the usual dishes served on rarely used china—food not only excellent but excessive as much for Dona Glória as for the other women, all of them now "of a certain age." Soup, a fish plate, a meat dish, fruit, dessert, tea or coffee.

Dona Carlota, a woman of little natural beauty, appeared bedecked in a splendorous dark red pomegranate dress and a bow at her waist in the fashion of the day.

"You know something?" Rosário later said to her brother. "They only use that room and the fancy dishes when the bishop comes."

Dona Glória wanted to know how life had been for José in all the time since she had cut his subsidy. He didn't hold back. In an irrepressible affirmation of his independence, almost to prove that he had survived by his own pluck after the cruel cancellation of the scholarship when he married Mariana, he did not hide any details. When he mentioned that he carried people's luggage to earn money to support his family, he heard two contradictory exclamations.

"Goodness gracious! How horrible!" Dona Carlota cried.

"Ah, how valiant!" old Dona Glória laughed.

"And what do you do now? What's your profession?"

José told them that after he finished his coursework, he became a private school teacher.

"I'm happy to know that, José. You can't imagine how happy I am. And do you have children?"

José mentioned how old his son was now, and that he had gone to work in Africa, and now was employed and earning enough to live on.

"And what does he look like?" Dona Glória asked.

"A nice-looking guy. He actually looks a lot like Amadeu," José answered.

At that memory, Dona Glória stayed silent a few moments. Then she said, "I'd like him to come visit me some day. I'd like to meet him."

After lunch, José went to his sisters' room and spoke with them privately. He asked them to tell him honestly what kind of inheritance Dona Glória was going to leave them.

"The inheritance," Rosário said, "is going to Dona Carlota. She goes around the house as if she's already received it. To us she's leaving a lifelong pension."

"That's all right," said José. "For my part, I will always help you out, as long as I live and, if we get another chance, I'll come visit you again."

Back home he spoke to Joaquim about Dona Glória's invitation for him to visit her.

"No, father. I'd like to see my aunts, but I'm not going to bow down in homage to a vast fortune."

Dona Carlota, a Dream Undone by Death

Gradually, more and more, Dona Carlota imposed her presence on House of Cedars as her aunt's heir. It was not enough for her to be recognized as such. Nor was it enough to have the best-appointed bedroom in the house, with exquisite furniture and mirrors that were almost improper for such a lady. More than once, rich landowners with their eye on fortune, had proposed marriage, but she refused. If she married, it would mean leaving House of Cedars with her husband. Naturally that wouldn't stop her from getting Dona Gloria's inheritance. But she would be stepping away from her position of heiress there, always present and vigilant. It would mean leaving Dona Glória in the hands of the two protected sisters who, as

Carlota saw clearly, were scheming to be willed the better part of the assets.

She did not dare reveal her concerns because Dona Glória, although old and shrunken, still herself and only herself ruled over her properties and the house. So Dona Carlota was alert and watchful over everything that happened, expecting to succeed the old lady in the great fortune of House of Cedars.

Everything was going in her direction except her health. One night she awoke with a violent pain in her chest, no ordinary pain but a sharp, unbearable pain that took her breath away.

She called out for help, awakening the servants, who went to inform Dona Glória, who said to wake the driver up and send him for the doctor.

The doctor came, observed the patient, who was still moaning in distress, gave her some pills to alleviate the pain and prescribed some medicine.

"You'll get better—in a matter of days. But you need to stay in bed for a while."

She was treated and got better, and returned to her usual life of waiting, year after year, for the old lady to die.

"You got quite a shock," Dona Glória told her with a hint of irony.

"Yes, it scared me," she agreed.

Life and death did not proceed in the expected manner. The old lady lasted many more years, moving around supported by her cane with the silver knob, an empress with her orders and reprimands.

And when it was least expected, Dona Carlota, the appointed heiress who was desperately waiting for Dona Glória to go before her, had another attack and died.

The great landowners in the region showed up in dark suits and ties, with the contrite demeanor appropriate for the circumstances, but without great lamentation. After all, it was only a candidate for the inheritance who had died. Despite her advanced age, House of Cedars would go on with Dona Glória at its head, a respected, admired lady and still the largest landowner in the region.

The funeral was one of great pomp and show with a big attendance. But there were few tears at the house.

What was sensible and contained in Rosário, Cristina had in imprudence. Sometimes she did not measure her words. Right after the funeral, she turned to her sister smiling, as if she had just heard good news. "You know something, Rosário? It was God who punished her."

After the funeral, Dona Glória called the two sisters in for a talk.

"Carlota is gone. You two are left. Carlota's sister Violante didn't come to the funeral. She'll only show up when I die to take charge of the assets. You, my daughters, are here now to keep me company. After I die, as I've told you, you'll have a fixed pension for the rest of your lives."

The "Lifelong Pension"

The old lady lasted yet another few years, but ended following the way of all mortals. It's not that she got sick: Her life simply snuffed out.

The other niece, Violante, immediately appeared. She had never set foot there during her aunt's life. She had made an independent life for herself. But now she came running, on the very day of the death, with the urgency of marking her presence as the heiress of the entire estate.

Once again, House of Cedars was decked in mourning.

The burial bespoke the wealth of the deceased and her justifiable renown as a benefactor. Many came from the families of great landowners. It was a sober funeral. The bishop spoke at the cemetery.

Real tears were shed by Rosário, Cristina, the servants and many of the poor the charitable lady had supported. The House of Cedars chauffeur, silent and servile, drove Dona Violante.

Dona Violante lost no time. She spoke to the two sisters. With the frigidity of a boss firing her maids, she told them that everything was set, and that within the week they would be taken by car to a home run by nuns.

In that moment the sisters sensed that something terribly unjust was about to take place.

They had come to that house as adolescents. They had spent many years there, almost their entire lives. They never had any suitors. They were too poor for the rich to want, and as they appeared to be members of the family of the house, the poor didn't dare to want them either. And now they had arrived at a point when their own old age was not far off. When Dona Glória died, Aunt Glória, they always believed their lifelong pension would allow them to live as they always had at House of Cedars.

Dona Violante arrived and right after Dona Glória's funeral she informed them she was putting them out on the street and sending them to a nuns' rest home. How was this possible? How could Dona Glória, so good, so charitable, so ready to extend a hand to people hit by misfortune, not have realized the cruelty of this treatment?

On the appointed day, very early, with their bags packed, the maids gave Rosário and Cristina their breakfast, alone. They served the usual dainty breakfast, making it clear there would be nothing more. Dona Violante never showed herself, nor had she even said goodbye the night before. The chauffeur was impatient, telling them more than once to hurry up, which they did. The servants helped them carry their luggage to the car and said farewell with hugs, kisses, tears and loving words.

"Dear ladies, what they're doing to you is not right. We will really miss you. With Dona Glória's death, everything will change. It will be other people, another house, and another life."

The maids were right.

For sure, some things would continue as before. The life of the rich would go on in a region where thousands of poor people lived. House of Cedars would still be a magnet sucking up money. The pitiful wages of the masses of lowly workers who came in from other regions to weed the rice fields would also continue. The miserable prices paid to the cork cutters would continue, while the latifundist would sell it on the market for a handsome profit.

But with Dona Glória's death the generous donations, the help for the poor, the prisoners' Christmas, the contributions to charitable organizations, all disappeared.

After Dona Glória's death, with the departure of the two sisters as though they were dismissed servants, and with Dona

Violante as the mistress of House of Cedars, everything would become different.

The maids were right.

The "Home"

During the two-hour drive the chauffeur didn't utter a single word. He transported Rosário and Cristina with complete indifference, as though he were moving merchandise. The sisters felt it. Even harder was the feeling of having been evicted from House of Cedars. They spent the whole trip overpowered by that sense. As the time of arrival approached, another image came to the fore in their minds: What would the nuns' rest home where they were being taken be like?

To their surprise, the car stopped in front of the gate of a beautiful palatial building with a pink façade.

They were expected. The gate opened, and the car entered, stopping before a large entrance door.

With the same indifference he had shown on the drive, the chauffeur got out of the car and didn't even help to lift the bags out.

Two nuns came running, their faces swallowed by their coifs and neckbands. They smiled warmly and spoke softly and gently. "Welcome, sisters. We'll help, we'll help."

And they did. They themselves wanted to carry the luggage and bags up a stairway, through corridors and halls, and finally into a room with a window admitting the morning sun. There was an armoire, two beds, two chairs, a little sofa and a table.

They asked if they had eaten breakfast and, after having their answer, if they might like to have anything, since the trip had been long and slow.

"Make yourselves comfortable, sisters. We'll come back. We're here to help you." And with that, they withdrew.

So began the residence at the nuns' rest home.

They could get up when they wished, they ate their frugal breakfast in the dining hall, returned to their room, possibly took a stroll through the garden, meals were at set hours, a chapel for prayer and mass. And thus the days began to pass.

Every day, every week, every month, always the same without exception.

Rosário and Cristina felt deeply despondent, with no desire for anything. They understood they had been sent to the "home" not so much to live but to end their days there.

Joaquim Visits His Aunts in the Convent

One day some nuns appeared at their room with unexpected news. A man with a youthful face had come to the gate saying he was the two sisters' nephew and wanting to pay them a visit. His name was Joaquim.

Joaquim, José's son! "Yes, that's our nephew. Have him come in," they asked excitedly.

Led to a small parlor, they ran to meet him.

They could hardly believe it. From the photos of Amadeu at House of Cedars, he looked just like him, handsome and attractive.

"It's exactly his face," Cristina said to her sister, "don't you think?"

They knew their brother had one son, but they knew nothing about him, what he did, what kind of life he led, if he was married or single, in short, what kind of person he was.

They asked so many questions and, to his own surprise, he began telling them everything about his life since childhood—a confession he had never made to anyone. About his failed studies, jobs he walked away from, his crazy antics, his going to Africa for work, his fantastic adventures.

The two sisters were spellbound. Joaquim brought them something new, an affirmation of life, a thirst for living, for fresh air, for space, for the world. Everything the young man recounted seemed like a fairytale. They used up the entire time allotted for the visit.

"Come back some more, Joaquim," they begged. "Your visit gave us so much happiness."

He promised, and he complied. Several times he came to relieve his old aunts of their final tedium and give them some compensatory moments.

José and Mariana Visit the Sisters and Reflect on Life

Joined by Mariana, José also visited his sisters. These were hours of tender affection. Since they were young, the only time they'd seen each other was that time José came to House of Cedars. All their lives they were so far from each other, unfamiliar with the way features had changed with the passage of years, nor how they were, how they lived and how they felt now. Yet all that time, overcoming such total separation, they felt like true siblings, connected by a profound, enduring love. Movingly, they shared stories about themselves that up to then no one else had ever heard.

Visiting time seemed to fly by, and at parting a deep empathy came out in words and gestures, as if translating the doleful foreknowledge that they wouldn't see each other again.

Returning home, José and Mariana spoke at length about the visit and the history of the family, a history of happy and unhappy times, of hard, punishing work and fascinating experiences, of contradictions and contrasts, of lives and deaths.

One day, in one of those conversations, Mariana made a surprising remark. "The world is haywire, don't you think, José?"

José agreed. "You're right, Mariana, it's haywire."

And little by little, as they continued the conversation over time, they started figuring out what was wrong with the world. And speaking of what was wrong, they went on to consider what was needed to make it better.

It was wrong having a few rich people with great fortunes and millions and millions of poor—extremely poor. Starvation wages were wrong. It was wrong for human beings not to get an education, nor even the possibility for it.

And flowing from those ills of a criminal world, they started imagining their ideal for a better one.

A world of equality for human beings, where no one would lack for bread and comfort. Where there was no more exploiting and dominating others. Where the great benefactor, rather than the rich, generous people as Dona Glória had been, would be society itself.

And another thing, which arose as the fruit of their own experience of life: A world where, in whatever situation or decision that had to be made, there was the love of freedom in people's spirits.

The family lived on. And the years passed, following the imperative law of nature: some whose lives ended, and others, descended from them, to ensure the future.

Photo: Eduardo Gageiro

A short biographical note on the author
Manuel Tiago

MANUEL Tiago was the pen name of Álvaro Cunhal. Edições Avante!, in Lisbon, has published nine titles by Manuel Tiago: *Até amanhã, camaradas* (Until Tomorrow, Comrades), which was adapted as a Portuguese television series in 2005; *A estrela de seis pontas* (The Six-Pointed Star); *A casa de Eulália* (Eulalia's House); *Fronteiras* (Border Crossings); *Um risco na areia* (A Line in the Sand); *Os corrécios e outros contos* (The Slackers and Other Stories); *Sala 3 e outros contos* (The 3rd Floor and Other Stories); *Lutas e vidas* (Struggle and Life), published together with The 3rd Floor; and *Cinco dias, cinco noites* (Five Days, Five Nights), adapted to film in 1996, which was the first of his works of fiction to appear in English. In its continuing series of Manual Tiago books, International Publishers has so far released *Five Days, Five Nights*; *The Six-Pointed Star*; *The 3rd Floor and Other Stories of the Portuguese Resistance*; *Border Crossings*; and now *The Slackers and Other Stories*.

Álvaro Cunhal was born in Coimbra, Portugal, on November 9, 1913. He began his revolutionary activity as a student at the law school (Faculdade de Direito) of Lisbon. He participated in the student movement and was elected in 1934 as the student representative to the University Senate. He was a militant in the Federation of Portuguese Communist Youth (Federação da Juventude Comunista Portuguesa), and was elected its secretary-general in 1935. In that year he went underground and participated in Moscow in the Sixth International Communist Youth Congress. He joined the Portuguese Communist Party (Partido Comunista Português, PCP) in 1931.

Arrested in 1937 and 1940, and subjected to torture, he returned to political struggle as soon as he was freed after several months in prison. He participated in the reorganization of the PCP in the early 1940s. Again living clandestinely, he was a member of the party Secretariat from 1942 to 1949.

Arrested anew in 1949 and brought before a fascist court, he delivered a ringing denunciation of the fascist dictatorship and a defense of his party's program. Judged guilty, he remained for 11 years in fascist prisons, almost eight of them in complete isolation. On January 3, 1960, he escaped from the prison fortress at Peniche together with a group of brave communist militants. Once again called to the Secretariat of the Central Committee, he was elected Secretary General of the PCP in 1961.

Living abroad, in Moscow and Paris, from that time forward he participated in numerous congresses and gatherings with communist parties and other revolutionary forces in international conferences. He played a critical role in organizing worldwide support, especially within the socialist countries, for the independence movements in the far-flung Portuguese colonies in Africa.

After the downfall of the fascist dictatorship on April 25, 1974, he served as Minister without Portfolio in the first four provisional governments, and was elected as a deputy to the Constituent Assembly in 1975 and to the Assembly for the Republic in 1975, 1979, 1980, 1983, 1985 and 1987. He was a member of the Council of State from 1982 to 1992.

In accordance with the decisions made at the 14th Congress of the PCP in 1992 concerning renewal and a new structure of leadership, he stepped down as Secretary General of the PCP and was elected by the Central Committee as President of the National Council of the party.

In December 1996, the 15th Congress of the PCP eliminated the National Council of the party and its presidency. Cunhal was re-elected as a member of the Central Committee.

He was re-elected to the Central Committee at the 16th and 17th party congresses in December 2000 and November 2004 respectively.

Under his own name Cunhal published several books about politics. He was a gifted artist as well: A book of his collected drawings has appeared. In addition, he published an original translation of Shakespeare's *King Lear*.

He died at the age of 91 on June 13, 2005. His funeral in Lisbon was attended by half a million people. He had one daughter, Ana Cunhal. The Portuguese government issued a postage stamp in his memory and later, in 2021, another stamp commemorating the centennial of the PCP to which he had devoted his life.

Photo: Eduardo Gageiro

About the Translator

ERIC A. Gordon, a Los Angeles resident since 1990, is a native of New Haven, Connecticut. His undergraduate degree is from Yale University, where he majored in Latin American Studies, studying Spanish five years and Portuguese two years. He also took a summer residency in Portuguese at New York University. He went on to Tulane University, where he continued studying Portuguese and wrote a master's thesis on the opera in Rio de Janeiro in the 19th century, using original sources uncovered in the Arquivo Nacional. He earned a doctorate in history, also from Tulane, writing his dissertation about the anarchist movement in Brazil in the pre-World War I era. He also studied Portuguese language and culture under a Gulbenkian Foundation fellowship in Lisbon.

International Publishers initiated its Manuel Tiago series in 2020 with Gordon's translation of *Five Days, Five Nights*, followed by *The Six-Pointed Star, The 3rd Floor and Other Stories of the Portuguese Resistance*, and *Border Crossings*. When complete, the series will comprise all nine works of fiction by Álvaro Cunhal, each appearing for the first time in English.

Gordon is the author of *Mark the Music: The Life and Work of Marc Blitzstein*, and co-author of *Ballad of an American: The Autobiography of Earl Robinson*. A memoir in short story form that he translated from Portuguese, *Waving to the Train and Other Stories*, by Hadasa Cytrynowicz, appeared in 2013 from Blue Thread Press. In 2015 he executive produced the compact disk *City of the Future: Yiddish Songs from the Former Soviet Union*, a collection of songs composed in 1931 by Samuel Polonski to the lyrics of major Soviet Yiddish poets. He is the author of a currently unpublished political autobiography.

From 1995 to 2010, Gordon was Director of the Workers Circle/Arbeter Ring in Southern California. He previously worked at Social and Public Art Resource Center, helping to produce murals all around the city of Los Angeles, which gave him the experience to commission a mural at the Workers Circle building. He was Southern California Chapter Chair of the National Writers Union (Local 1981 UAW/

AFL-CIO) for two terms. He has written for dozens of local, national, and international publications, mostly about art, music, culture, and politics. From 2014 onward, he has been a staff writer and editor for *People's World* online newspaper.

From 2006-09 Gordon took coursework toward certification as a Secular Jewish Leader, referred to in Yiddish as a *vegvayzer*. Upon graduation, he became a legal officiant certified to conduct weddings and other ceremonial functions, a role equivalent in law to a minister, priest, or rabbi. He has a similar endorsement as a Humanist celebrant for people of any background. For five years he served as a Deputy Commissioner of Civil Marriage for the County of Los Angeles, where he conducted 1500 marriages.

Eric A. Gordon can be contacted at ericarthurgo@gmail.com.

Questions to Ponder and Discuss

IN "The Slackers," we see that the officers try to isolate the open Communist from the other "correctional" soldiers. When Reinaldo and Braga return to the base having been discharged from further service, how do you suppose that happened? A payoff? Politically sympathetic judges on the Medical Board? Or perhaps just the final realization that these two never could and never would conform to military life?

What do you make of the mysterious character Afonso the cook, the one who never tells his story and seems to have a privileged relationship with the officers?

It's interesting that, apart from the title story and "Délinha," the three other stories might have included obligatory military service as part of these portraits of Portuguese life. It doesn't come up much in his other books either. Why do you suppose the author ignored this factor in so many families' lives?

"Hand in Hand" obviously takes place after the 1974 Revolution that freed Portugal from the grip of fascism. Were you aware that the Soviet Bloc nations—in this story, likely the USSR itself—offered courses in Marxist education to students from so many different countries?

"Parallel Stories" talks about Party life not under conditions of clandestinity, but in the open atmosphere of the post-1974 period. The author exposes various tendencies that emerged in the Communist Party, and how they were dealt with. Did you find any parallels to people, or to ideological positions you may have encountered in your own political experience? Was this story helpful in guiding the reader toward productive ways of handling dissent, and of organizing for social change?

"Délinha" sounds like it might have been based on a true incident, either in the author's life or something he heard about. In many ways it seems out of character with the rest of Manuel Tiago's writing. But is there a "social" message in this story? Is it possible to read the adorable child as a metaphor for the hypnotizing attractions of a consumer society and the way we blame ourselves for the ways we are seduced by it? How can we account for the way Délinha seemingly gets away with her grievous folly without even an apology and without punishment? Or should the reader just conclude, this was a six-year-old girl who just wanted to get back to her parents? It may not be true to the actual incident, assuming the story is based on one, but why couldn't one sensible adult go back up the mountain and tell the narrator, "Hey, you can come down now. The kid's okay." Finally, is there even some humor in the way the narrator gets so overwrought?

The description of José, the history teacher in "Lives," with his unorthodox and highly humanistic approach to history, education and psychology, leads a reader to believe he has profound class consciousness, yet he doesn't seem to be active in any political party or movement. Nor is he especially successful raising his own son Joaquim. Only at the end, with his wife Mariana, do they start imagining what a better world might look like. What do you make of this?

One of the ancestors of José's mother-in-law was Ferreirinha, the conservative Miguelist dating back to the 1830s. Why did the author include this historical anecdote? Just for its amusement value? Or do you think he used it to show that the conflict between liberal and reactionary ideas has a long history and is still playing out to this day?

Joaquim seems to enjoy his visits to his aunts, or at least take satisfaction in the pleasure these visits give them. Do you think this signals a turnabout in his character?

The two sisters are sent to a grim convent rest home to end their days. Do you think Dona Violante altered the terms of their "lifelong pension," or is this what Dona Glória had planned all along? If the latter, does that change your estimation of her famous benefactor status?

And what do you make of the author's assertion that the two sisters were deemed either too rich or too poor to find husbands? Perhaps that is just what Dona Glória wanted to believe—and wanted them to believe—so that she could have their companionship as long as she lived. Considering her close and generous relationship with the Church, couldn't she easily have put out the word about their marriageability, and perhaps even have helped the young couples a bit if they needed it? In the end, did she really do them much of a favor by taking them in?

The final paragraph of "Lives" reads: "The family lived on. And the years passed, following the imperative law of nature: Some whose lives ended, and others, descended from them, to ensure the future." Clearly, the author is talking broadly about the human family, yet did you realize that this particular family did in fact die out without descendants? João had no children, and his death is not mentioned—unless Joaquim had children that we don't know about. Was this an oversight on the author's part, or did he mean to make some point?

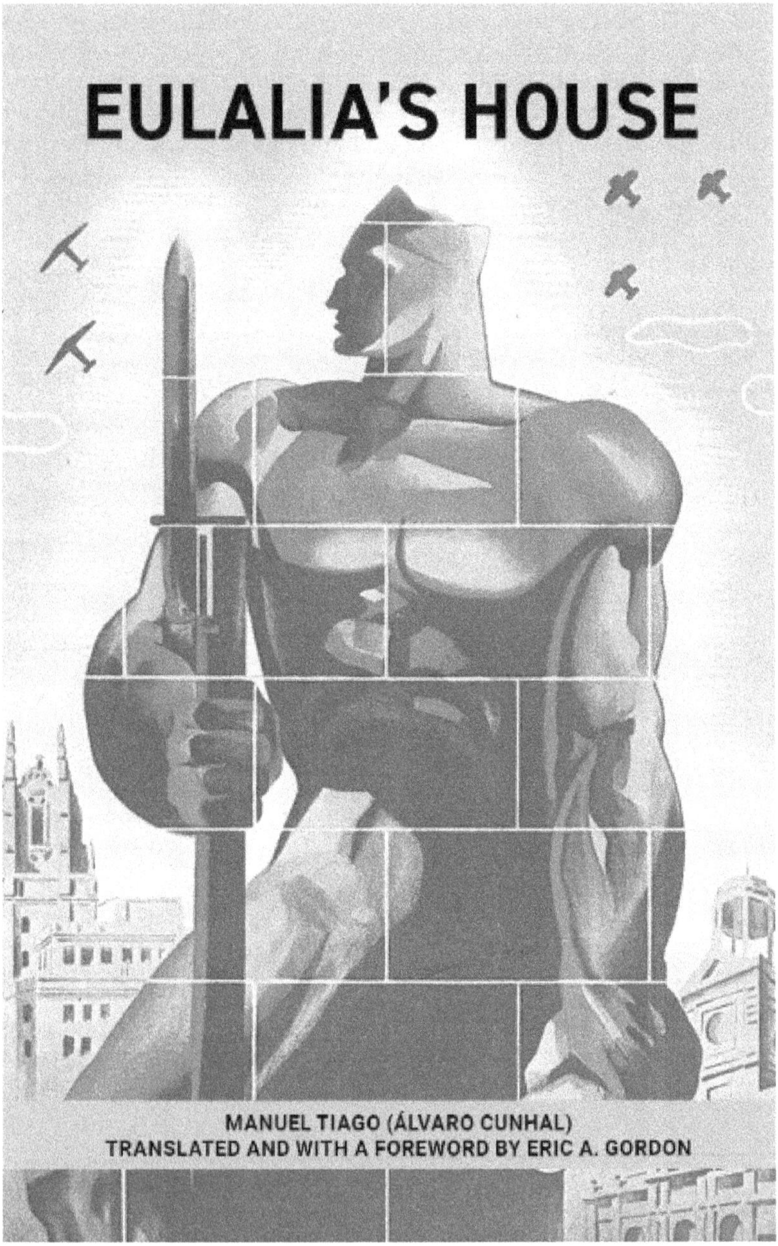

EULALIA'S HOUSE

MANUEL TIAGO (ÁLVARO CUNHAL)
TRANSLATED AND WITH A FOREWORD BY ERIC A. GORDON

Forthcoming from International Publishers: The next book in the complete fiction of Manuel Tiago

Eulalia's House

(*A casa de Eulália*)

Chapter I

Seated at an outdoor café in the old city, the three comrades conversed and sipped their cool draft beers, whose flavor seemed heightened by the intense heat in the air. Their drinks were the same, but their manners distinct. António was attentive, looking from one side to the other as if expecting something sudden to occur. Manuel watched all around, pleasurably following the girls walking by. Renato, with his leg lazily stretched out, seemed absentminded, barely joining the conversation with just the odd word or two.

To a casual observer brought there from afar with his eyes blindfolded then abruptly uncovered, the circulation on the street, the sidewalks full, people moving about, groups standing in the buildings' shadow—all would seem normal for a Sunday like any other Sunday in summer there in the center of the city, not far from the Puerta del Sol.

So it looked in that corner, in that moment, at first glance. But with prolonged observation, new and strange things could be seen. It was new and unusual that cars would pass by from time to time, interrupting the restful quietude with horn blasts and shouting. It was strange that many men and women prominently wore caps of various styles with letters and insignias. Stranger yet, hearing from nearby streets cracks like the bombs at the Santo Antonio festival, they listened more closely and held still.

At just the moment when António was commenting on the tranquility of their locale, one of those cracks rang out, and the young man, casting a glance toward the end of the street, saw people quickly converging in one place and standing in a group. He said, "It could be, they have killed another person."

Like other émigrés, he spoke in a mishmash of half Spanish, half Portuguese. They had acquired the habit as the most practical for Portuguese people: Everyone would understand them.

"Maybe," Renato said without expression, taking another swallow of his beer.

Maybe, but not certain yet. In recent weeks there had been an increase in attacks on militants and newspaper hawkers on the left. Some had been killed.

On that street, in that moment in the old city, everything was more or less tranquil. But Madrid was a boiling volcano.

Demonstrations and confrontations took place every day. Cars drove by at crazy speeds, their occupants shouting slogans, unfurling their party flags which waved freely in the air. Here and there gunfire broke out, yet curiously, rarely did people chase after anyone.

Rumors spread of a military coup in preparation against the government of the Republic. It was said that the fascists had revolted at the Cuartel de la Montaña, and had closed off the garrison gates to outside contact.

To a nearby Spaniard at the next table, the situation was clear. "If the coup takes place, they are gonna get fucked."

All right, that was one prediction. So for them, the three Portuguese political émigrés sitting there, what would they do in case of a coup?

António worked mornings in a car repair shop. Directly tied to the Party, he performed a very particular task. Knowledgeable as he was about the frontier, usually he was tasked with receiving underground comrades from the Portuguese side and talking them to Madrid, and organizing return trips across the border from Spain to Portugal.

In recent weeks he had been in regular contact with a prominent comrade whom he had picked up at the border. He had come with a special mission which António only partially knew: to secure the freedom of two other comrades who, on crossing the border at the Guadiana River, had been seized by the Guardia Civil, brought to trial for transporting arms, sentenced and imprisoned in Huelva. The comrade never told him his name, and he didn't ask. To António he would remain simply The Comrade, and that's how he referred to him.

Manuel did not yet have a settled life. He had arrived only recently, following a dangerous incident with the youth movement. He hadn't thought about what to do in case of a fascist coup, but he had a general feeling: "I don't know for sure, but I won't be standing around with my arms folded."

Renato assumed a divergent position. He had taken part in the famous workers' strike in Marinha Grande on January 18, 1934. As he was well known in the area, he hid out in the Leiria pine forest. With his wife, he managed to leave Portugal somehow and now they were working—she as a domestic, and he as a shop employee, though it had closed a few days earlier.

"If they have a coup, that's their business. I came from Portugal to stay out of trouble; I didn't come to Spain to get mixed up in more here."

Since António retorted that such a position didn't sound like him, Renato added, "Yes, it does. If I want to make trouble, there's plenty to do in Portugal."

And so they talked that afternoon. It was already twilight before they said goodbye. Renato went to Las Ventas at one end of the city. António and Manuel both went to Puerta del Ángel at the other end, as they were both lodged at the same house.

That was Eulalia's house, as they called it.

Lightning Source UK Ltd.
Milton Keynes UK
UKHW012026050922
408363UK00001B/120